The
JUMBIES

The
JUMBIES

Tracey Baptiste

Layla Alkaki

ALGONQUIN YOUNG READERS   2016

To my children, Alyssa and Adam,
without whom this book
would have been finished years ago.

And to all the children of the
Caribbean (no matter your age).
See, you have fairy tales too.

Published by
ALGONQUIN YOUNG READERS
an imprint of Algonquin Books of Chapel Hill
Post Office Box 2225
Chapel Hill, North Carolina 27515-2225

a division of
Workman Publishing
225 Varick Street
New York, New York 10014

First paperback edition, Algonquin Young Readers, April 2016.
First published in hardcover by Algonquin Young Readers in April 2015.
Printed in the United States of America.
Published simultaneously in Canada by Thomas Allen & Son Limited.
Design by Carla Weise.

LIBRARY OF CONGRESS CATALOGING-IN-PUBLICATION DATA
Baptiste, Tracey.
The jumbies / Tracey Baptiste.—First edition.
Summary: Eleven-year-old Corinne must call on her courage and
an ancient magic to stop an evil spirit and save her island home.
ISBN 978-1-61620-414-3 (HC)
[1. Spirits—Fiction. 2. Magic—Fiction. 3. Blacks—Caribbean Area—Fiction.
4. Caribbean Area—Fiction. 5. Horror stories.] I. Title.
PZ7.B229515Ju 2015
[Fic]—dc23   2014038605

ISBN 978-1-61620-592-8 (PB)

10 9 8 7

1

The Forest

Corinne La Mer's heart beat like wild drums as she ran through the forest. Her bare feet stumbled over the dead leaves and protruding roots of the forest floor. She strained her eyes in the dappled sunlight to keep track of the small, furry agouti that scampered away from her. Occasionally, light glinted off the smooth rock tied to the animal's hind leg. It called to Corinne like a beacon. When she got close enough, she pounced on the 'gouti and missed, grabbing only a handful of dirt. Corinne grunted and threw the dirt aside. The animal ran beneath a bush and Corinne squeezed down to the damp earth to crawl after it. Her skirt got caught on branches, but she ripped it away, determined to reach the animal. On the other side, the creature cowered against a rock and the roots of a large tree. In her eleven years of life, Corinne had learned that with nowhere to run, a wild animal might try to attack. She hung back.

"I'm not going to hurt you," she said in her calmest voice. She eased closer. "I just need that thing on your leg. You'll be able to run much faster without it, and I won't be chasing you . . . so . . ." She moved with care toward the 'gouti and gently untied the silk cord. The animal's coarse fur shivered and its pulse beat as fast as her own. Corinne closed her fist firmly around the stone pendant and crawled back out of the bush.

She rubbed the stone with her thumb. Over years of constant handling, she had worn a smooth groove that fit her finger perfectly. The pendant had been her mama's, and when she put her thumb into the little hollow, she imagined her mama's hand around her own. Corinne breathed a sigh of relief now that it was back in her possession, but her relief did not last long.

She didn't know this part of the forest. And it was darker here. The branches of the mahogany trees were so thick that barely any light came through. It even smelled different, of wood and wet earth, while Corinne was used to the smell of the sea. She had no idea which way was out.

Somewhere between the leaves, Corinne thought she saw a pair of lights shining. They were close together, like eyes. Her skin prickled, but then the lights disappeared and Corinne tried to shake off her fear. The little bit of light must have been reflecting on something. *Don't be silly,* she scolded herself. "I'm going to kill those boys," she muttered into the heavy air.

A pair of yellow-bellied birds alighted on a branch overhead, and called out, *kis-ka-dee kis-ka-dee!* Something small scratched through the undergrowth. A cold lump formed in Corinne's stomach and began to spread. She had heard grown-ups tell stories about the terrible things that lived in hidden pockets of the island, like this forest filled with ancient mahogany trees. They talked about creatures with backward feet, and women who could shed their skin, and women with hooves for feet. Even though her papa told her these stories were not true, there must have been a reason no one ever came this far into the forest.

Corinne felt the wind at her left cheek. She followed it as her papa had taught her to do.

After a few minutes, the trees thinned out. There was a bit more sunlight filtering through the branches. Corinne breathed easier. Her heart slowed its pace. But she continued to hurry over the uneven ground, ducking beneath trees as she went. Then, behind her, the bushes rustled. She turned just in time to see something move in the shadows. Surely it was only an animal. But what if it was another kind of thing entirely? The kind of thing from the grown-ups' stories?

A *jumbie*.

The hairs on her arms stood on end. She gripped her mama's necklace as she glanced behind her. From a curtain of shadow, the two large yellow eyes blinked. Corinne turned and ran as fast as she could. The thing snarled and rushed after her.

Corinne concentrated on the ground as she fled. She burst through the last line of trees onto the dirt road. A large pair of hands grabbed her. Corinne squeezed her eyes shut.

"What are you running from, Corinne?" a familiar voice asked.

She opened her eyes, relieved. "Nothing, Papa," she said. Her breath came in fast sips and her body shook.

Pierre La Mer looked into her eyes. "Why were you in there?"

Corinne looked down the road. Near the dried-up well, two boys in tattered, dirty clothing stood watching them. The older one was smiling with mischief. He held a small frog in his hands over the top of the well. It was struggling, but he held it firmly. *Their next victim,* Corinne thought. Corinne let the stone pendant dangle from her fingers. Its smooth surface gleamed. The smile slid off the boy's face. The younger one looked surprised and then his face broke into a grin. His brother nudged him hard.

"Those filthy boys tied Mama's necklace to a baby

'gouti and scared it into the forest. I had to get it back, didn't I?"

"What boys?" Pierre looked around, but the boys had run away. "You actually chased an agouti into the forest and caught it?" He looked at Corinne from head to foot and pulled some of the twigs and leaves from her braids. Suddenly, he laughed. "I've raised a hunter!" He kissed both her cheeks, but then his face grew serious. "You should be old enough to know not to go running in the woods. There are wild animals in the bush, Corinne. There's a reason you don't see anyone else in there."

Corinne looked back at the bushes and thought of those shining eyes and the thing that had run after her.

Her father swept her up into a tight hug. "Your heart is going quicker than a riptide. Did something frighten you? It wasn't a jumbie was it?" he teased.

In her father's arms, in the open air, Corinne laughed at her fear. She hugged him back and said, "No, Papa."

"Of course not. Nothing frightens my girl, right?" He winked. Pierre wiped some mud off his daughter's face. "The sun is going down. It's time to go visit your mama. Are you ready?"

Corinne retied the necklace around her neck and felt the stone settle close to her heart. "Ready."

Corinne and her father walked away as the sun slipped toward the horizon.

They did not see the pair of yellow eyes that brought

a dim light to the edge of the forest. The darker it got, the brighter the eyes became. The eyes watched Corinne and Pierre as they went on the road until they disappeared around a bend. And once the sun descended beneath the tops of the trees and the forest shadows lengthened along the road, the jumbie emerged.

Corinne wanted to retriver her moms necklece but the boys tied it to an agouti, so corinne had to chase it down.

2

The Graveyard

Corinne and her father joined dozens of other people walking to the graveyard. It was an All Hallow's Eve tradition to pay respect to those buried there. Many people on Corinne's island believed All Hallow's Eve was the one night when the dead had the power to seek out the living. Some said spirits and jumbies came out to exact revenge on those who had wronged them. Of the two, people of the island feared jumbies more. In the stories people told, jumbies lived among people, hidden in the shadows, always waiting for their moment to attack, mostly out of pure wickedness. Most believed in them, but Pierre had taught Corinne that spirits and jumbies were all nonsense. So while some children clung close to their parents, Corinne was not afraid. She skipped ahead of everyone and began to sing.

Ti-dong, ti-dong dong, ti-dong
Crapaud tingele
The frog is hopping, hopping, hopping, hopping
Crapaud tingele

A few of the braver children joined her.

Ti-dong, ti-dong dong, ti-dong
Crapaud tingele

As the crowd got closer to the churchyard their song trailed off. Children returned to their parents, and Corinne felt her father's large hand close around her own. Fresh sea air was in his long, locked hair, and the sharp scent of saltwater wafted out of his damp sandals as he walked. His hands were warm and rough from working on the sea, pulling in his nets full of fishes.

The old stone church came into view at the top of a low hill. Corinne could just make out the whitewashed tombstones and wooden crosses in the graveyard next to it. Her eyes moved over the crowd. There was Laurent, walking next to his mother, both with the same sun-baked skin and wide eyes. Lucia and her brothers walked ahead of their mother and father. Lucia's mother panted and tried to keep up, though it was hard with the weight of her belly filled with Lucia's latest brother or sister.

"I remember her, you know," Corinne told Pierre. "I remember my mama."

"Do you?" Pierre asked with a smile.

"She had thick black braids that fell down the middle of her back."

"Like yours?"

"Just like mine," Corinne said with a smile. "And her skin was the deep brown color of earth."

"Just like yours!" Pierre said.

"Yes. And her eyes were as round and bright as the sun."

"Hmm, and how do you remember all of that?"

"You tell me every day, Papa!" Corinne said.

Pierre's laugh mingled with the sound of waves that rolled back out to sea. Pierre and Corinne quickened their pace and entered the churchyard just as the final rays of sunlight threw an orange veil over the world.

"Orange magic," Corinne and her father said together.

"Your mama's favorite time of day," said Pierre. His eyes filled with tears.

mom did

"Then we're here at just the right time," Corinne said. She squeezed his hand and pulled him past the people who were already in the small graveyard, lighting candles and planting flowers. In a corner near a sapling tree, Pierre traced his hand over the words carved into a wooden cross.

His hand lingered longest over "Nicole."

He plucked a white orange blossom from the sapling tree and tucked it into Corinne's hair. It still had the strong scent of oranges even though it had already begun to fold its petals in for the night. Corinne remembered when they had buried her mama in the ground like a seed. Corinne was four years old, and her mama had been teaching her to grow things. At the burial Corinne had whispered, "How long will it take for her to grow back, Papa?" But the look on his face told her that not everything that was put in the ground would give something back. A little orange tree had appeared next to the grave a year later, and had bloomed every year since, but it was not the same as having her mother.

Pierre took some candles out of his pocket and struck a match. He passed the flame under each candle. As the wax melted, he pressed the candles into the hard ground over the grave and lit each wick. The flames flickered with the sea breeze.

"Look, Papa," Corinne said, pointing toward the sky. "Like fireflies."

Pierre had just looked up at the hundreds of flickering yellow flames hovering over the dark graveyard, when their light was eclipsed by a large man.

"The spirits are out tonight, my friend," the man said. His voice boomed over the tombstones as he clapped Pierre on the back.

"Hugo!" Pierre said with a smile. "How are you doing?"

Hugo nodded. "I'm doing all right." He patted himself, and as he did, little wafts of fresh flour puffed off his clothes. Hugo was the village baker. He always smelled of fresh bread and had dough beneath his fingernails. Even his cheeks puffed out like pastry. Hugo touched his unlit candle to one of Pierre's. The flame doubled in size, then split into two as Hugo pulled his candle away. "The dead walk the earth, little one," he said to Corinne. "Aren't you afraid?"

She touched her mama's stone pendant, smiled at her father, and shook her head.

Hugo laughed. The sound carried over the graveyard and brought all eyes to their little corner. He pulled at one of her shiny black braids. "Not afraid of the dead, but are you afraid of losing? The other children have already begun their collections."

Corinne looked at the balls of wax the others were gathering. This was the game they played while the grown-ups cleaned the graves and chatted among themselves. The one with the biggest ball of wax at the end of the night was declared the winner and had the right to gloat on the walk home.

"I have another idea," she said. She reached for the

nearest candle and pulled away the soft wax that dripped off the side.

"Mind the clear wax, Corinne!" Pierre warned.

Corinne ran to join the children who moved among the graves, scooping up handfuls of dripping wax and balling them up in their hands. Older children like Corinne knew to touch only the wax that was turning a cloudy white. The little ones either burned the tips of their fingers on the scalding-hot transparent wax that was just falling, or waited too long and tried to break off the already-cooled hard white pieces.

After they had visited all the graves, Corinne's friends left the churchyard with lumpy grayish balls of candle wax in varying sizes, but Corinne did not.

"Did you win?" Papa asked.

"Mine's not a ball." She had shaped her wax into a woman with long braids just like hers. She showed it to her father.

He touched the wax figure gently. "You still should have won. Yours is pretty big."

"I don't mind," Corinne said. "This is better." She looked at her friends Lucia and Laurent, who hefted lumpy wax balls larger than their hands. They looked at her and grinned. Corinne held up her statue and smiled back.

"Still not big enough," Laurent said.

"Not bigger than mine," Lucia said.

Everyone held on to their wax collections like prizes,

though Lucia had been declared the winner. She went skipping ahead, but she had to keep stopping for her mother.

As they all streamed back out to the road, Pierre stepped toward a woman who was standing alone in the shadows. "Are you lost?" he asked the stranger.

The woman turned toward him and slowly shook her head. Corinne could only make out the woman's face in the darkness. Her eyes reflected the moon like quicksilver.

Pierre hesitated as if he wanted to say something more to the woman.

"Papa!" Corinne called to her father. He returned to her side. "Look, Papa," she said. She held up her doll against the moon. "It's glowing."

Pierre smiled. "It must be magic . . . like you." Corinne followed her father's gaze as he looked back toward the shadows, but the woman was gone. All she saw now was the empty graveyard.

I think its a jumbie.

3

Sister

As the voices of people faded in the distance, the jumbie moved out of the protection of the shadows and prowled on all fours over the freshly cleaned tombs. The low, flickering candles lit her naked body as she sniffed at each grave. Her eyes reflected the light back as though they were candles themselves. Her limbs were thin and as gnarled as branches. As she moved, the air rustled against her body.

The rustling stopped as she came to the grave by the orange sapling tree. She smelled the scent of the man who had stopped to talk to her. Pierre, they had called him. And just like Pierre had done earlier, she traced her hand over the name on the wooden cross. She did not recognize it. Her kind did not use markings like these. But she was drawn to something in the scent that arose through the decay and the rotting wood and wormy soil beneath. She had recognized some of that scent on the child earlier, the one who had come running into the forest, the same one with a wax figure that resembled her sister.

She whispered into the ground, as gently as the sound of wind through the leaves. "Is that you?" Her language was known to the animals, plants, rocks, and other jumbies, but not understood by humans. "You never came back. I never knew what happened to you."

There was no answer, only the sound of waves crashing in the sea.

"Did you give up your sissy for that child? She looks like she has lived for as long as you have been gone. Did they kill you? Or did you die from being separated from us?" She pressed her cheek against the ground, and sang:

Sister, sister mine from birth
Rotting now beneath the earth

Mingled bodies, mud from mud
Forever lost to human blood.

Sister mine since time began
Sleeping underneath the sand

One is lost but one is found
A family broken, now made sound.

A low rumble emanated from the jumbie's chest. It grew louder and louder and ended in a shriek that pierced the air. People in nearby villages heard the scream, but comforted themselves with the thought that it was an owl on the hunt, even though it sounded like no owl they had ever heard before. Muddy tears flowed down the jumbie's hollow cheeks. As they touched the ground, they turned into centipedes that scattered over the graves. When she stopped crying, she rose to her feet and said, "Hush, hush, now sister. We will see if we can be a family again."

The jumbie crept along the outskirts of the island through the frothy sea to where the water grew calm and warm. There the open mouth of a swamp rolled from deep inland, meandering through a thick mangrove forest with still, slick water. The jumbie walked into the swamp and followed it to a muddy island. An old shack sat askew on it, its boards rotting with damp and falling away from the rusty nails that struggled to keep it together.

The jumbie called out. It was a low, throaty sound, nearly indistinguishable from the croaking of nearby frogs—the *crapaud* from the children's song—except that it pierced the air like an arrow. The witch who owned the little shack heard the jumbie's call at once, even though she was standing a mile away from her home. The witch was crouched over a patch of white mushrooms, catching the magic that only came in the three hours after midnight. She swatted away the sound of the jumbie's call like a mosquito at her ears and continued with her work.

When the witch did not answer her call, the jumbie's eyes flashed with anger. She broke into the shack and took some small bottles filled with the witch's medicines. Then she wrapped her bare skin in a length of green cloth and returned to the trees.

Who is caring
Sister? Dose the witch
interact?.

4

Market Day

The scent of oranges filled the house as Corinne was gently shaken awake by her papa.

"Today is the day," he said to her sleepy face. "Your oranges are ready for market."

Corinne breathed in without opening her eyes. "Yes, I smell them."

Corinne and Pierre had the best soil on the island. It was why Corinne's mama, Nicole, had chosen that spot near the forest for their home. Their garden was always bursting with blooms and fresh fruit and vegetables. And today, finally, the oranges were in.

"You are growing up. Your oranges will help you to

make your own way and then you won't need your old papa anymore."

Corinne smiled at their game. "What would I do without you, Papa?" she asked, peeping at him beneath her thick eyelashes. "Who will tell me that the ocean is too big for me to swim in alone? Who will tell me not to climb trees and skin my knees? Who will tell me that I put too much salt in that fish?"

Pierre laughed. "I guess you need me after all." He kissed the long tight braids on her head and brushed her soft skin with the back of his hand. "Watch your purse in the market," he said.

"Watch the sea doesn't swallow you up," she said.

"I have seawater in my veins," Pierre said. "And anyway, if the sea swallows me up, it will spit me back out again. You know how the sea is. Nothing stays at the bottom forever."

"Except for Grand-père," Corinne said. "The sea kept him."

"Grand-père wouldn't have it any other way. He is king of the fish-folk," Pierre said. "And that is why you will always be safe in the sea."

Corinne breathed the cool morning air that washed up from the shore. Most fishermen lived right on the coast, and everyone else who lived in villages scattered throughout the island stayed far from the mahogany forest, but Corinne and her papa lived on a hill nestled among the

< 19 >

outer edge of the forest trees overlooking their fishing village. That was where Corinne's mama had liked it, close to the forest. It was where she grew things. It was where she was happy.

Jumbies

It was still inky dark before dawn, and in moments, Corinne could no longer see her papa as he walked toward the sea. But after sunrise, the sea would become a clear blue with hints of green deep beneath. Then, the tips of rippling waves would sparkle in the sunlight, making the sea almost blinding. But Corinne's papa was used to the sea. He grew up there. Grand-père had been a fisherman, too, and spent most of his days out on the boat with his nets, like his father before him. Corinne's papa had taught her everything he knew about the sea, but she was not going to be a fisherman. Corinne breathed in the scent of her oranges. She was like her mama. She belonged to the land.

As Pierre walked down to his boat, Corinne turned back to her pillow, thinking of her grand-père swimming among the fishes. When Corinne finally got up, the sun had risen but barely penetrated the thick layer of clouds that hung over the island. From the living room window, she could spot her father's bright yellow boat reflecting what little light there was back to shore. He had painted his boat just so that Corinne could spot him easily from the house and know that he was still near.

Instead of the usual colorful cotton skirt and white

blouse that most of the girls on the island wore, Corinne got dressed in some of her father's old clothes. She used rope to tie the pants tight around her waist and rolled up the hem to her ankles and his shirt sleeves to her wrists. Satisfied that she looked very grown-up and business-like, Corinne went out to pick the best oranges to sell. Their garden was filled with fruit and vegetables, most planted by Corinne's mama before Corinne was born. There were guava and pomerac, peppers and tomatoes, cassava, dasheen, and chives, each neatly planted around the garden, but in the middle was the orange tree. Corinne remembered her mama's hands over her own, pushing the seed into the ground. She remembered watching it as it sprouted up and its leaves uncurled in the sun. The little plant grew with her and then shot up past her. Now, it reached over even her papa's head.

As Corinne worked in the garden, the memory of her mama holding the small white orange seed came to her mind. Her mama had told her that the seed was magic. *If you take care of it, it will take care of you,* she had said as she taught Corinne how deep to plant the seed, and how much water to give it. Pierre reminded her of all the things her mama used to say, but Corinne could never remember the sound of her mama's voice. When she thought of it, she only heard the sound of the wind through the leaves. That morning, Corinne could almost feel her mother's hands on hers, and she could smell her mother's woody scent. *A seed is a promise, Corinne, a guarantee. Plant it and watch it grow.*

When Corinne's basket was full, she tied her long braids behind her head with a colorful piece of cloth and wrapped another cloth around the basket handles so they wouldn't hurt her hands on the way to market. She walked down the dusty path to the main road and went past the edge of the forest. Pink and red hibiscus held their petals open to the sun while bees took advantage of their pollen. When she paused to switch hands, a hummingbird hovered near her basket for a moment. It seemed to drink in the scent of her oranges before it darted off. Already, the day was getting hot. The farther Corinne got from the sea, the less breeze there was to cool her. By the time she reached the dry well, the sound of seagulls and waves had become the sound of chirping birds and animals running through the bushes at the sides of the road. Past the next well—the full one—and a few houses just outside of town, the sound of the market arose. The hum of people haggling over prices, the chickens squawking, and the cries of goats and pigs filled the air. Then came the smells—ground spices, ripe fruit, and strong coffee among them. Corinne didn't hesitate at the entrance of the market. She walked straight in and staked out a spot in the crowd. She rolled out the cloth from around her hands and spread it on the ground. Then she began to arrange her oranges in pyramids of five on top of it.

"Oh no, no, no, child," a woman selling eddoes said. "You can't set up here. This is my spot." She was small and brown with short wiry hair just like her vegetables had.

Corinne stood up to her full height, which only got her as high as the woman's shoulders. "There aren't assigned spots," she said sharply.

"Go somewhere else, darling," the eddoes seller said. Her lips smiled, but her eyes were as hard as pebbles.

Pebble eyes put her hands on her heavy hips and a tall woman with dry, ashen skin stood up next to her to back her up. Corinne had seen her father deal with rivals before. She stood her ground. But a little way behind them, another woman, selling peppers, smiled at Corinne and beckoned her with a quick flip of her wrist. The pepper vendor folded the edge of her blanket in order to make room. Corinne narrowed her eyes at pebble eyes and her flaky-skinned friend but decided to squeeze in next to the lady with the peppers.

"Thank you," Corinne said as she began to set up. Her new market neighbor was wearing a bright yellow sari and her hair draped behind her like a black silk curtain.

"Don't mind them," the woman said. She raised her voice loud enough for everyone to hear. "Nobody's buying their rotten vegetables anyway."

Pebble eyes sneered and grumbled under her breath. Flaky skin sucked her teeth, *chups*. Corinne smiled at her neighbor, who had soft-looking arms, just the kind that

Corinne would have liked to feel folded around her. A small face peered around the woman and startled Corinne. The face disappeared almost as suddenly as it had shown up. Corinne felt a deep pang of loneliness when she realized that her neighbor had come to the market with her child. She tried to shake off the feeling. "I have the sweetest oranges on the island," she said.

"Very good," the woman in the sari said. "You'll get a lot of customers, then."

The market bustled with people haggling about money and the quality of produce. Coins dropped into hands and jingled in pouches. Vendors sang about their wares over the steady hum of negotiations.

"Sweet, sweet figs here! Get your sweet figs!"

"Potatoes for stew! Cheap for me! Plenty for you!"

"Nice ripe melongene! Ask Miss Jen for melongene!"

"Long mango! Sweet mango! Julie mango! Sweet mango!"

And then the market voices fell silent. The hush began at one side of the square and rippled out to every corner. A beautiful woman moved past market-goers in the suddenly still crowd. She was dressed in a green cloth the color of forest leaves. Corinne pushed through elbows to get a better look.

The cloth wrapped around her body flowed behind her. She walked with such grace that she appeared to be gliding along on a ribbon of green. Her skin was the deep brown color of wet soil. Her hair was piled high on top of her head in a yellow, blue, and green cloth. She paused briefly and turned. Corinne felt as though the woman looked right inside of her, and her heart leaped in her chest. But it was impossible to tell who the woman was really looking at from her deep-set eyes outlined by thick eyelashes as black as shade.

Corinne kept her eyes fixed on the woman as she walked through the market. As she passed, the crowd found its voice again.

Some held out their produce for her to buy. Those who didn't narrowed their eyes and whispered about her behind their hands.

"Who is she?"

"All my born days and I never saw that woman before."

"Anyone know who her people are? There's no way to tell what kind of person she is without knowing her family."

The woman in green finally stopped far from Corinne, in front of an ancient woman with striking white hair, who sat beneath the only tree in the market.

She had come to see the witch.

I think that the witch is going to be a jumbie.

5

The Green Woman

The white witch did not look up from arranging her magic on the blanket.

"I need something from you, old woman," the jumbie said in a low voice.

The witch snorted. The short white braids on her head twitched. "You took what you wanted from my hut last night. Look how you're using it to fool these people into thinking you are a regular woman. So what else you need from me?" The witch moved another vial of her smelly potions.

"You did not have enough of what I needed."

"Oh no?" the witch asked drily.

"I plan on a long visit."

That made the witch look up.

The jumbie smiled. "Oh yes, a very long visit."

"I can't help you," the white witch said. "I can't help one side at the expense of the other."

"You did it before," the jumbie reminded her.

The white witch shook her head. Her braids tossed in every direction. "That was different. That was for the benefit of both sides. I can't intervene like this. If I help one, I have to help the other. For balance."

"You have been helping their side for years!" The jumbie gestured at the bottles and pouches on the witch's blanket.

"These?" The witch laughed. "You know as well as I do that these concoctions don't do nearly as much as they think."

A growl started in the jumbie's throat. Her voice became rough. "You will help me, old woman."

The witch bared the few yellow teeth she had left in her mouth. "Go back to the hole you came from. Wait there, and see if I will ever help you."

The jumbie turned to leave, but tossed one last threat over her shoulder. "You will help me, or you will suffer."

Corinne's mom was the Jumbie.

6

Drupatee Sareena Rootsingh

As the woman in green exited the market, the vendors and customers put their heads together to discuss the beautiful new stranger.

"What did she want with the white witch?" asked the woman with pebble eyes.

"Same as everybody wants with the white witch," said her tall neighbor. "Help with man trouble."

"How could a woman who looks like that have trouble with a man?" pebble eyes asked.

"She is very beautiful," flaky skin agreed.

"Maybe it's a man she shouldn't have."

The two women looked at each other and then at the

road that the woman in green had taken. They shook their heads and went back to their work.

When Corinne returned to her oranges, a very small girl was standing there, eyeing them hungrily. She was the girl who had peeked from behind the woman in the yellow sari. The girl was wearing a dirty pink sari herself, and her pitch-black hair hung in two slick, heavy braids past her waist. "How much?" she asked, pointing to Corinne's oranges.

"Ten," Corinne said.

"Are they sweet?"

"They're the best on the island. You can try one if you like, but you still have to buy it."

The girl gently smoothed the end of one of her braids. "I'll buy all five."

Corinne took the coins from the girl and put them in her pouch, then looked back across the market to where the witch was sitting.

The girl followed Corinne's gaze. "My mother says the white witch is trouble." She peeled off orange rinds and dropped them at her feet. She took a bite. Her eyes widened with surprise. She took two more quick bites, and Corinne was happy to see that her first customer was so pleased.

"My papa says that people are afraid of things they don't understand," Corinne said. "How does anyone even know she's really a witch?"

< 29 >

"Do you see all those bottles and powders she has on her blanket? There's magic in them. They can make things happen."

Corinne picked up a discarded seed from the ground. "There's magic in this too. Does that make me a witch?"

The smaller girl's eyes widened again. "Are you?"

"Of course not!"

The girls watched as the witch sent another customer off with a bottle and a piece of paper.

"What kind of magic does she do?" Corinne asked.

"I don't know."

Corinne looked the girl up and down. "Then how do you know it's really magic?"

"Customers don't come back to you unless you sell them what they want. My mother says that the white witch has been sitting there for as long as the oldest person on the island can remember. Whatever she's selling works. You can tell by the way her pouch jingles at the end of the day. And I know that what she is selling is not for cooking." The girl licked sticky orange juice off her hands. "That was the sweetest orange I ever had."

Corinne smiled with satisfaction. "Thank you. They're from the best soil on the island. Right next to the mahogany forest."

"Really?" the girl said. "You grow your oranges near the forest?" Then she shrugged. "I guess that's why you could chase that 'gouti into the forest. You're used to taking risks."

"You saw that?"

"Mmm hmm. I was going to the well when I saw you run in. I stayed a little while to see if you would come out, but my mother was waiting. I'm glad you made it back out alive."

"My papa told me I have nothing to fear from the forest."

"Even that forest? Your father must not know very much then," the little girl said.

"What he knows is that most people are afraid of made-up stories," Corinne snapped back. When she saw the girl stiffen, she quickly added, "Anyway, I had to get this back." Corinne pulled the necklace out of her shirt and showed off the shining stone. "It was my mother's."

"Well," the girl said, "I still think you were lucky, considering the day. Everybody knows if there's any day you shouldn't go into that forest, it's All Hallow's Eve—the spirits and jumbies are roaming. Ask anybody."

Jumbies. Corinne remembered the yellow eyes in the forest and her heart beat hard against her chest. She forced out a laugh to drown out the sound. "There are no such things as spirits and jumbies."

"You shouldn't say that." The girl's eyes darted around to see if anyone—or anything—was listening. "Just because you don't believe doesn't mean they're not there."

"If these jumbies are all around, how come nobody has ever actually seen one?" Corinne asked. "The forest is dangerous because there are wild animals, not because of jumbies." She set her jaw and folded her arms. "Anyway, I wasn't the only one in the forest yesterday. I saw a farmer."

Yes, Corinne thought, *it was just a farmer.*

"How do you know? It might have been a jumbie, like a *lagahoo*. Did you hear it howl like a wolf? Chains rattling? Probably not. They say if you are close enough to hear his chains, it's already too late for you." She looked at Corinne eagerly for an answer.

Corinne laughed a little more easily this time. "No. It was quiet. No howling or chains rattling."

"Then it could have been a *La Diabless*. They say the devil woman is very pretty. Did you see her face? Or was it a short jumbie? Those are *douen*. You can't see their faces either. And you should never answer if they call."

A confident smile broke out on Corinne's face. Nothing in the mahogany forest resembled any of those creatures. "Nothing like that." She watched the look of disappointment cross the girl's face. "But it was too dark to see much," she added. "What's your name, anyway?"

"Drupatee Sareena Rootsingh," said the little girl. "You can call me Dru."

"I'm Corinne. Corinne La Mer."

Dru's eyes narrowed. "Can I tell you something? My mother tells me all the time that if you don't trouble trouble, then trouble won't trouble you."

"That's good advice," Corinne said. "I'll start taking it tomorrow. Today I have to get back at those boys."

"The ones who took your mother's necklace? What are you going to do?"

Corinne grinned.

I think that corinne is going to go in the forest and find a Jumbie.

7

Down the Well

A small frog sat hopeless at the bottom of the dry well. It was tired from trying to escape and hoarse from croaking. It was the croaking that had gotten it into the well in the first place. If it had just been quiet, the boys would not have found it and dropped it in. The frog wished they had at least dropped it into a full well. Drowning in freshwater had to be better than dying of thirst in a deep, dark, stone hole. If the frog did not get wet soon, it would not survive.

Something dripped down on the frog from the circle of light above. The moisture sank into the frog's flesh and revived it temporarily. Then a rope slid down the wall.

The sweet smell of dirt and oranges seeped into the frog's pores. Something blocked the light from the top, something that was getting closer. A few minutes later, a girl stood at the bottom of the well holding on to the rope and looking at the frog with glee.

"Hello, Mr. Crapaud," Corinne said. "I've come to rescue you."

Corinne scooped up the frog in one hand and put it in her pocket. Then she tried to pull her way up on the rope with her feet pushing against the wall. Although the well was mostly dry, some moisture remained in the rocks. The cracks between them were slick with moss and fungus. Corinne slipped and banged into the wall as she tried to scramble up. More than once, the frog got squished between her hip and the side of the well. It croaked pitifully.

"Crapaud tingele," Corinne sang in an effort to soothe it. She pulled up on the rope, but her foot slipped again and sent them both slamming into the wall and then back down to the bottom of the well.

More croaking.

"Shh!" Corinne scolded the flattened frog. "This is hard enough without your constant complaining, and we have to hurry. Those boys will be back to torture you any minute."

After a few more attempts, Corinne figured out how to grab on to the crevices with her fingers and toes. She knew not to move to a new spot until she was secure. Once she

< 35 >

had the hang of the slippery rocks, she barely needed to use the rope. It was too hard on her hands, anyway.

Once they were outside of the well, another drop of Dru's salty tears fell on the frog's back. It was the most water it had in an entire day.

"I told you not to worry," Corinne told her new friend. "I said we'd get back out just fine." Corinne picked up a half of a coconut shell from the ground and poured the rainwater inside it onto the frog's skin. She set the animal down. The frog hopped quickly toward the forest. It turned around at the edge of the trees and watched the girls. Then it turned back and hopped out of sight.

"Now we put these in," Corinne said, pointing at a wriggling sack on the ground.

Dru shied back a few steps.

"It's okay. You just have to know how to handle them."

Dru became slightly yellow with fear, but stepped carefully up to the writhing sack and held the ends with her fingertips.

"Be careful not to drop it," Corinne said.

Dru nodded and squeezed her eyes closed. Corinne untied the sack and gently emptied its contents, nearly a dozen scorpions, into the well. The scorpions fell with a series of tiny thuds at the bottom, and in an effort to escape, they immediately began to climb the rope.

"Come on, they'll be here any second." Corinne hid in some thick shrubs near the edge of the forest.

"Don't get too close!" Dru said. She fingered the end of her braid nervously.

"I told you, there's nothing in there," Corinne said looking over her shoulder at the forest. She shuddered despite herself. "Fine. I'll find somewhere else for us to hide. But only because you are so nervous." Corinne led Dru across the dirt road and they both crouched inside a thicket of tall grass.

At their usual time, the brothers appeared around the bend in the road. They picked up a few stones and fitted them into their slingshots. Then they went to the well.

What will happen to the frog?

8

The Brothers

"Where are you, Mr. Frog?" Bouki shouted into the well. He pulled back on his slingshot and let a stone loose down the well. He looked in again. "Hiding, eh?" His tattered shirt flapped in the wind.

Dru shifted next to Corinne, causing some rocks to scrape the ground. Bouki turned to scan the bushes. At one point he looked straight in their direction. Corinne grabbed Dru's hand and held her breath.

Bouki went back to looking down the well. In the light, Corinne noticed an intricate pattern beneath the grime on Bouki's shirt, a pattern that showed the shirt had once belonged to someone wealthy, maybe, but now was doing the work of keeping a boy's back from the sun.

Malik, the younger brother, walked in a circle around the well. As he walked, he kept tucking his unruly curls behind a pair of ears that seemed too big for his small head. Corinne tried not to giggle when he found the rope tied to the trunk of a small tree. Malik waved his brother over.

"Yes, it's a rope. So?" Bouki asked. Then he rolled his eyes. "Frogs don't climb ropes, brother."

Malik put his hands on his hips, jerked his curly head toward the forest, and waited for his brother to understand.

Bouki shook his head at his little brother and sighed. "You mean, it was that girl? I bet she climbed in and got the frog."

Malik chuckled a little.

"It's not funny, big ears. She's spoiling our fun. But at least she left us some rope. We could always use it for something."

Malik pulled the rope up as Bouki peered into the well to see the end of it.

Bouki kept his slingshot ready for anything that came out, but he barely noticed the small insect that scrambled up the rope and out of the well. Soon there was another and another. Bouki jumped back. "Scorpions!" he cried out.

Malik dropped the rope and ran to his brother. There

< 39 >

was a scorpion hanging on to Bouki's tattered shirt. Malik grabbed a pebble and his slingshot and shot at the scorpion. He just grazed the insect, and it reared its stinger above Bouki's arm. He grabbed another stone and shot it off again just as the scorpion's tail was coming down. The insect flew with the pebble and disappeared into a nearby bush.

"You saved me, little brother," Bouki said as he panted with relief.

Malik merely tucked his hair behind his ears and breathed another long sigh in response.

The girls tried to smother their laughter as they crawled out of the grass. Corinne walked up to the boys. Halfway there, she caught a scorpion by the tail, immobilizing it so it couldn't use its stinger. "I thought I'd give you something new to play with," she said.

Bouki turned toward her. His face was red with anger. "That could have killed me!"

"Not this little one," Corinne said. "It would have hurt pretty bad, though." She chuckled. "How about you sending me into the forest? Some animal in there could have killed me."

"There's nothing in there that can kill you. Scratch you up, maybe. Anyway, you didn't have to go," Bouki said. "I didn't force you."

"You knew I would. *You* didn't have to come to the well to torture the frog."

"You knew we would," Bouki said.

"So we're even then." Corinne tossed the scorpion away.

Bouki nodded. He spat in his hand and held it out for Corinne to shake. She hesitated for a moment but did the same, and they pumped hands until Bouki noticed the little girl behind her. "Who's that?"

"That's Dru," Corinne said.

"You're the marketplace thieves," Dru said.

"What? Thieves! What have you ever seen us stealing?" Bouki asked defiantly.

Malik stomped his foot in agreement.

Dru suddenly looked uncertain. Again, she fingered the end of her braid. "I've seen you take food at the market," she said quietly. "Clothes too."

Bouki smoothed his shirt over his chest. "Oh yeah? Why haven't we ever seen you?"

"She's sneakier than she looks," Corinne said. "And she's usually with her mother."

Malik pulled up the tail of Bouki's shirt and pretended to hide behind the cloth.

Understanding dawned on Bouki's face. "Oh, you're that one!" he said smiling. "Do you sleep with your mother too?"

"I have nightmares! Anyway, I'm not with her now," Dru said.

"And she helped me with the scorpions," Corinne added.

Dru stuck her chin out boldly. "That's right. I did."

"So you traded hanging on to your mother's skirt for hanging on to this one's pants?" Bouki frowned and looked over Corinne's market-day outfit. "What are you wearing, anyway?"

"How is that your business?" Corinne fired back. "And what about him?" she jutted her chin toward the smaller boy. "Does he ever talk?"

"Of course he talks. That's a stupid question."

"Well," Dru said, "are you being mean because you just got tricked, or is it because you have no people?"

Bouki sucked his teeth, *chups*. "You mean like a mother and father? What do we need people for?"

"For getting some decent clothes, for one thing," Dru said with a glance at their tattered shirts and pants.

"Your friend here doesn't look much better in her old-man getup," he said, pointing at Corinne. "And what we have is fine for us."

"If you had a mother she would never let you go out like that." Dru said.

"We take care of ourselves," Bouki said.

"I don't have a mother either," Corinne said. She moved slightly toward the boys. "Where do you live?"

Bouki pointed toward a muddy group of hills in the distance. "Over there, mostly, but wherever we find shelter."

Malik's eyes narrowed at the look of shock on Dru's face.

"My brother thinks you're very insulting," Bouki said to Dru. "Besides, not everyone needs a house. It's better to sleep under the stars. The night air is good for you. It makes you strong."

Right on cue, Malik flexed his muscles.

"What do you do when it rains?" Corinne asked.

Bouki shrugged. "Then we have a bath."

"Well get ready for a long shower," she said, glancing up at storm clouds rolling in. "It's about to pour."

"We better go home," Dru said. She already held the loose end of her sari over her head even though the rain had not begun to fall yet.

"We've got a great spot for waiting out a storm, don't we brother?" Bouki said. "It's better than either of your houses, I bet."

"So show us, then," Corinne said.

"If I'm not back in time for supper—" Dru began.

"Poor baby has to be back for milk, eh?" Bouki teased.

"I'm not a baby!" Dru shouted.

"Then stop rubbing your fancy meals in our faces and let's go," Bouki said, and he started off toward the hills.

Dru looked up the road in the direction of her village and then back at the other three children. She hesitated.

"You don't have to come if you don't want to," Corinne said softly.

"No, I'll come with you," she said. Still, it took a couple of seconds for her feet to move.

The brothers led Corinne and Dru away from the road along a path that only the two of them seemed to know. They went behind the market and cut through the yards in a small village, shooing chickens and ducks in their path, and bobbing under wet laundry that was getting wetter as the rain began to fall. After the village, they came to a wooded area. This was not as dense as the old mahogany forest that Corinne knew from the center of the island. These trees were farther apart with more light between them and more air wafting around their trunks. Just as the rain began to come down in large drops, the brothers stopped at an old tree with branches and leaves so thick that the rain could not get through its canopy. The four sat against its trunk as the rain soaked everything around them.

"Do you like living on your own?" Corinne asked the boys.

Malik intertwined two of his fingers.

"We're not alone," Bouki added. "We're together." He wrapped his fingers together too. "It's just like you and your father. Do you feel like you're on your own?"

"Living with a father is a bit different from living with a brother," Corinne said.

"He isn't just a brother. He's *my* brother. And that's plenty," Bouki said.

"I have six older brothers and sisters," Dru said. "And a father and a mother."

Corinne imagined a house with that many people inside. "That must be nice," she said.

Bouki shook his head no. "That is too many."

Corinne said, "I bet it's never lonely with so much family around all the time."

"It's never quiet either," Dru said with a laugh.

The patter of raindrops slowed and finally stopped.

Bouki stood. "I think I should show you the quietest place on the island. Perfect for when you want to get away from someone." He eyed Malik. And Malik gave him the same look back.

"How far is it?" Dru asked.

"Follow me," Bouki said. When Dru hesitated again, he added, "Don't worry, you'll be back with your mommy before you know it."

They followed Bouki until they heard the gentle rushing of water, which grew louder the farther they walked. At a break in the trees they found a river that cut a meandering path through the island. At a small tributary, they drank deeply, ignoring the tadpoles and small lizards that darted through their fingers. The boys pulled out their slingshots and felled a few bright red pomeracs. They ate the sweet fruit as they went single file, following the trickling offshoot to the main river. There, the water was deep and narrow enough that they could swim from one bank to the other, but wide enough that they didn't want to. Except for the gentle rustle of leaves that surrounded the river and the rippling sound of the water as it skipped over stones, everything was silent. They all stopped and waited, drinking in the sound of nearly nothing. Sunlight appeared and pierced through the overhang of leaves to glitter on the surface of the green river. It cast rippling light on the smooth rocks of the riverbed. The air became steamy as the sun began to suck the moisture out of the island, and suddenly the river was an oasis that none of them could resist.

Corinne was the last of them to dive in. Before she did, she felt the skin on the back of her neck prickle. It was just like the day before in the mahogany forest. She shivered and looked behind her. But there was no one there. She thought they were alone.

She was wrong.

forshadowing

I think its
a water jumbie.

9

Watching

The jumbie hid in the bushes as the children crossed her path. She watched each of them, especially her sister's child.

"Last one in's made of lizard guts!" the taller boy said.

The smallest boy held his nose and pointed to his feet. The others squealed, "No, stinky feet!" and ran down to the river. But it was the small, quiet boy who flipped from a rock into the river before the rest of them. Her sister's child had hesitated before she joined the others, and the jumbie watched them tease her for it.

The jumbie listened to the sound of their laughter and the sound of the water lapping against their skin. She watched them dive under the water and then come back up for air, gasping if they had stayed too long beneath the surface. She understood her sister's fascination with people: their brown skin and dark eyes, even the clumsy way they moved.

The little girl and her father were more graceful than most. The jumbie had found their house earlier and watched them go about their morning. The man was especially graceful when he was on the water. His muscles rippled beneath his sun-darkened skin as smoothly as rolling waves. He was certainly interesting. She would take care to observe the man and child up close, to understand how they had lured her sister away from her own kind. She wanted to understand this before she decided what to do with them.

The children floating on the water reminded her of the men who had come to the island long ago on large wooden islands they called ships. The ships had bright cloth that billowed above them like stiff clouds. It was marvelous the way they moved. She remembered how she swam out to greet the sailors but gasped when she realized it was trees they had cut down to create their ships. The sailors had attacked her as she climbed up the hull. When she fought back and pulled the men under the waves, they gulped the water, sending up smaller and smaller bubbles of air, until their bodies went as limp as weeds.

The children are just like those men, she thought, *perhaps even more fragile.*

The jumbie crouched lower. A small red lizard scurried out from the grass. She caught it in her fingers and shoved it into her mouth. As she watched, other lizards passed by. She picked them, one by one, and had them for snacks. She drew on their energy and gathered enough strength to change. Her skin took on the mossy green color of the tree trunks around her. Except for the green cloth that was wrapped around her body, she was now nearly indistinguishable from her surroundings. Transparent. She tugged at the cloth and let it slip to the ground and hid it under a rock. Then she crawled to the edge of the river. As she went, her skin took on the color of everything she passed: dirt, stone, tree, grass. She was like a ripple of water moving closer to her target. She sat on a stone in the muddy shore, completely invisible to the children. She would be able to observe them up close. Then she saw the witch on the far shore. As silent as a breath, the jumbie slipped into the water. She took her time diving deep, then swam beneath the playing children and stood on the riverbed beneath their kicking feet.

The jumbie planned her attack. *Who should I take down first?* Their legs paddled above her head. She decided on the biggest one. The boy. She pushed off from the bottom and glided upward. Her fingers reached toward his toes.

like a chamelion

why dose She want to Attack

10

In the River

"Did you feel that?" Bouki asked. He looked around at a frothy ripple that had sprung up by his elbow. "I felt something."

"Your own shadow pulling your leg?" Corinne asked with a laugh.

"Look, my fingers are turning wrinkly," Dru said.

"If you stay in the water long enough, your whole body turns wrinkly like that," Corinne said. "You'll look like the white witch."

"Didn't anyone feel that?" Bouki asked again.

"Feel what?" Corinne asked.

Bouki swam around in a circle and peered at his legs waving frantically in the water. "Something touched my feet."

"Don't tell me you're afraid of a little fish," Corinne said. She looked over at Dru, who giggled, but started to look more cautiously at the water.

"That was no little fish," Bouki said. "It would have to be very big."

Dru stiffened. "How big?"

"Big enough to pull my foot."

"Fish can't pull," Corinne said.

Dru looked at the clear water around her and thought she saw something moving beneath them. "We should get out of the water," she said. "It's getting late and I have to get back home."

"It's nothing, Dru," Corinne said.

"You think everything is nothing," Dru replied.

"There it is again!"

"Stop screaming, Bouki!" Dru cried.

"You're screaming too!"

As the others thrashed around, only Corinne and Malik remained calm. They rolled their eyes at the other two, and Corinne splashed water at Malik, which left sparkling drops of water at the end of his curls. But then Corinne felt something herself. And she was sure, just as Bouki had been, that it was no fish.

"Hush, both of you. Let's just swim to another part of the river." Corinne turned to swim off, and as she did, she felt something brush against her leg again. She stopped midstroke and looked around.

"What is it?" Dru asked. "Did you feel something?"

Corinne nodded. "Maybe he was right." The girls gulped air and swam straight to shore.

They will See another Jumbie. And they will get hurt.

< 52 >

11

Balance

The old witch had heard the children splashing in the river and looked out at them. She caught the eye of the jumbie just as she turned herself invisible and moved toward the water. *"Chut!"* the witch whispered to herself. She did not like to get involved. But when the bigger boy started looking around as if something had touched him, the witch dove into the water at once. The color faded from her body as if it had been washed away by the river. In seconds, the witch was as transparent as the jumbie herself. And she reached the jumbie faster than any river fish could swim.

The witch rammed into the jumbie through the children's feet and pulled her fast and hard back down to the riverbed. She held the jumbie there, pushing her into the sand. The jumbie managed to get her feet under the white witch and pushed up as hard as she could. The witch lost her grip and the woman swam up toward the children again.

The witch could only make out the outline of the jumbie's body as she cut through the water, but it was enough for her to follow. And now the witch was furious. She knocked the jumbie away from the children. The jumbie turned and dug her bony fingers into the witch's flesh. She bore down hard. The witch raised her right arm and struck mightily at the jumbie's chest. At the same time, she felt a sharp pain as her other arm snapped in two.

Both the witch and the jumbie floated away from each other as the children made their way back to shore. The witch had saved the children. But immediately, she realized what saving them meant.

From shore, Corinne, Dru, Bouki, and Malik watched the water in the middle of the river churn. When it stopped suddenly, and the last ripple broke on the bank, they waited in silence for something else to happen, but nothing did.

"I want to go home," Dru said.

< 54 >

"Wait," Corinne said. Her teeth chattered either from cold or fear. But the rest of her body didn't move.

"Dru's right," Bouki said. "Why are we waiting for whatever it is to come out?"

So they all moved away from the water, but Corinne still watched. After a few moments, the witch surfaced on the far side of the river, sputtering. Her color had returned, so the children could see her clearly. With only one good arm, she struggled to reach the shore. She looked weak and ancient.

Dru saw Corinne's muscles tighten. "No!" she cried, but it was too late. Corinne had already dived back into the river and was swimming to the witch. "She tried to kill us!" Dru shouted, but Corinne could see that the witch was hurt.

Corinne was a good swimmer, though not as strong or as fast as her papa. When she reached the old woman, she grabbed her around the waist and pulled her the rest of the way to the opposite shore. The witch winced when Corinne touched her arm. Corinne took care not to touch it as she propped the old lady against a rock to sit.

"Stupid children!" the witch said. She swatted Corinne's arm away. "What are you doing here, anyway?"

"I'm helping you," Corinne snapped. "If I hadn't re-alized that it was a drowning person grabbing at us, we might have left and you would be dead for sure."

"Get away from here," the witch said through gritted teeth. Then she yelled across the river. "Go home to your mothers!"

The witch's words stung Corinne like a lash against her skin. "You nasty, old—" Corinne began. But a furious look from the witch made the rest of her words dissolve in her mouth. Instead, Corinne turned and dove back into the river just as her tears began to fall and the burning sensation in her throat caused her to gasp. She swam as quickly as she could, gulping air every few seconds, so by the time she reached the other side, her friends easily mistook her red eyes and panting breath for tiredness from the swim.

Corinne ran off with the other three behind.

• • •

With the children gone, the witch breathed more easily. She relaxed against the rock. On the opposite shore, the jumbie returned her body to its visible form and wrapped the green cloth around herself.

"You know what happens now," the jumbie shouted across the river. "You helped them. Now you have to help me." She laughed out loud. "Balance!"

The witch muttered a curse under her breath.

I think the witch is going to want the children for help.

12

Two Houses

The boys retreated to their cave in the hills, so Corinne walked a frightened Dru back to her village, a small collection of wooden houses in the middle of fields of cocoa, sugarcane, and figs. It was evening now, and the farmers, covered in sweat and soil, were just returning from the fields with the satisfied look of work well done on their creased faces.

A group of people—Corinne counted seven—all with Dru's large almond-shaped eyes and thick black hair, came down the road laughing and arguing.

"You smell like dung, Arjun! Have you been playing with the cows again?" a tall girl asked.

"How do you know what I smell like, Fatima? Can you smell anything over that stink coming from your armpits?" The boy shoved the girl, and she kicked dust into his face.

"Aye, watch it!" a smaller boy shouted. "You're quarreling with him, not me."

"Who can see you there?" the tall girl asked. "You're too small to be walking with the rest of us."

"Yeah, Karma, why don't you go to market with Mami and the baby," another small one said.

"I'm not a baby!" Dru said. She twirled the end of her hair in one hand and curled the other hand into a tight fist. "You're not one year older than me, Vidia."

Vidia and the rest of Dru's siblings looked down at her and smiled. "Where'd you come from?" Karma asked. "You're done playing in the market?"

"Are you done playing in the field?" Dru shot back.

Fatima, who looked like the eldest, raised an eyebrow. "You're getting fierce. Pretty soon you won't be hanging on the back of Mami's sari anymore, eh?"

"She was with me most of the day," Corinne said. "Not with your mami."

"This is my friend Corinne," Dru said. "Corinne, these are my brothers and sisters. And that's my father at the back."

A tall, thin man wearing a homemade straw hat smiled at Corinne, then tipped his hat.

"A friend, eh?" Fatima asked. "Why are you dressed like that, Corinne?"

Arjun shoved Fatima in the arm and said, "Maybe she has those chicken legs like yours. They're easier to hide in pants."

"They're my papa's clothes," Corinne explained. "It's what he wears to sell. And today I was selling at the market, so . . ."

"So that getup is for business?" Fatima said with a nod of understanding. "So people won't give you any trouble, eh?"

"You think she can't handle trouble?" Arjun asked. "Look at her. She looks like she brings the trouble herself."

Corinne grinned.

When they all got to the house, Dru's mother, Mrs. Rootsingh, came out with her hands on her hips. "What took you all so long? Dinner is almost dried up from sitting in the pot." When she spotted Corinne, her face softened. "Are you staying for supper?"

"No, Miss, my papa will be expecting me," Corinne said.

"At least have something to drink before you walk back," Mrs. Rootsingh said.

The girls followed her to the back of the house and watched as the goat let out a bleat of surprise when Mrs. Rootsingh began to milk it. Corinne and Dru waited as Mrs. Rootsingh went into the kitchen and came back with two warm cups of foam-covered milk. Instead of handing them to the girls, she hesitated on the unvarnished top step. "I thought Dru only brought one friend!"

Dru and Corinne turned around. Just behind them was a small boy, no older than six.

"Oh look, it's your tail," Arjun called out from a window. "Come to wag?"

"Stop that, Arjun. Why don't you go wash the dung off yourself," Mrs. Rootsingh said sharply. She handed the milk to Dru and Corinne and went back to get another.

Dru handed her cup to the boy, who immediately took a sip that left a line of froth on his top lip.

The middle brother snickered. "Drink up, babies."

"Who are you?" Corinne asked the little boy.

"I'm Allan," he said.

"I'm Corinne," she said. "Nice to meet you."

"He lives over there," Dru said to Corinne. She pointed to a ramshackle house across the street.

Mrs. Rootsingh returned with the third cup of milk. The three of them sipped their milk and listened to the clamor of the rest of the Rootsingh family, talking, laughing, tossing things around.

At a brief dip in the noise, Mrs. Rootsingh said, "The sky is turning dark again, Corinne. You'd better head home before you get caught in the storm." The wind picked up suddenly, and Mrs. Rootsingh's sari flapped against the bare wood walls.

Corinne downed her milk and thanked Mrs. Rootsingh. Dru's mother took the cup and turned to go back inside. As she did, a piece of her sari caught on a nail and ripped off. Corinne pocketed the smooth piece of cloth. She froze when Allan's mouth opened as if he was about to say something. Both of their eyes flashed to Dru, who was still sipping and looking out at the goats. Corinne put her finger to her lips. Allan closed his mouth. Then Corinne darted off down the dirt road.

"Don't let the jumbies eat you!" Arjun shouted after her.

"Oh shush!" Mrs. Rootsingh snapped. "Why don't you . . ." Whatever else she said was lost to the wind.

• • •

As soon as Corinne lost sight of Dru's house, it began to rain again. By the time she got to her house, the sun had set, and her clothes were soaked. She stopped a moment outside her house and took out Mrs. Rootsingh's bit of sari cloth. It slipped around the tips of her fingers, smooth and soft. She went to the orange tree and said, "Mama, this is my friend's mother. You would have liked her." She dug a hole and buried Mrs. Rootsingh's sari between the roots.

As Corinne turned toward her house, a memory came to her of walking on small, pudgy feet through her house toward the open back door. She could see the ocean through the door and hear the waves crashing outside.

Seagulls dove through the air and cried. She could even hear the leaves shaking in the wind. Just before she reached the door, her mama scooped her up in her arms. Her mama's mouth moved, telling her something, but her voice was lost in the sound of the seagulls, the waves, and the wind.

Corinne blinked, and the vision of her mama was gone. She walked inside, expecting to see her father reading by lamplight. The voices she heard coming through the open kitchen door were a surprise. As she crossed the threshold, she saw her father leaning near the stove by a small pot of boiling water, laughing. Beside him was the woman in green.

"Hello," the woman said.

"Corinne! Where have you been in all this rain? You're soaked." Her father ran toward her with a kitchen cloth. "How did you do at market today?"

Corinne untied the pouch from around her waist and dropped it on the kitchen table with a jingly thud.

"I heard your daughter's oranges were the sweetest anyone had ever tasted. There weren't any left by the time I was ready to buy," the woman said.

"Corinne, this is Severine," Pierre said.

"I saw you in the market," Corinne said. "You didn't seem to be looking for any oranges."

Severine's eyes darted to Corinne's father and then back to Corinne. "I had some business to take care of. But

I came back later and you and your lovely oranges were gone." She smiled.

Corinne looked at her father. "You know her?"

"We met at the wharf today," he said. "She came to buy fish, but she didn't get there early enough. Then when the rain started to pour down, I invited her to stay here until it was over."

"There are more oranges on the tree. I could get you some now if you want," Corinne offered.

"I would certainly pay you for them," Severine said.

Corinne saw her father frown a little at Severine's suggestion of money. "No charge," she said.

"Thank you."

"It's still raining, Corinne. Maybe you can get them later," Pierre said.

Corinne shrugged. "I'm already all wet." She ran out quickly, picked two of the closest oranges to the house, and returned to the kitchen. She cut one of them in half and squeezed some of the juice into the tea her father was brewing for himself and Severine.

Pierre took a sip. "It's perfect," he said. "It makes you feel good from the inside out."

Severine's eyes lit up when she took her first sip as well. She gripped the cup and slurped up the rest of the tea in several loud gulps. Then she shifted her eyes from Corinne to Pierre, who had fallen silent watching her. Severine wiped her mouth and said, "You have a talent."

Corinne was still dumbstruck, so Pierre nudged her a little. "It's not me," Corinne sputtered. "It's just a seed in the ground growing the way it should."

"But not every seed that is planted brings such beautiful fruit," Severine said. "You made this happen. Accept the part that you play in it."

"She's right, Corinne," Pierre said. He turned to Severine. "You should see the way she tends to the trees, making sure there are no pests, blowing warm air on them when the nights are too cold."

Corinne's face flushed, and she smiled despite herself. "I learned it from my mama."

Severine nodded. "Of course you did. Is that her?" She pointed to the wax figure on a shelf in the other room.

Corinne nodded.

"She made that too," Pierre said with a wink at Corinne.

"You must miss your mama. I know what that is like to lose someone suddenly." She reached her hand out toward Corinne, but Corinne did not take it. After a moment, Severine let it drop back to her side.

Pierre said, "Corinne, you should change out of those wet clothes before you get sick." He leaned over and kissed her on the top of her head, then pushed her out of the kitchen.

When Corinne returned from changing, Severine was standing at the door. "It stopped raining," she said to Pierre. "I think it's time I went home."

"Can you make it back in the dark?" Pierre asked. "You don't have a lantern."

"I know these paths like they're written on my hand," Severine said. "Thank you for letting me keep dry in your house, Pierre." She looked at Corinne. "Maybe you will save me some oranges tomorrow?"

"You will be at the market again?" Corinne asked as she squeezed more water out of her hair into a towel.

Severine glided out into the darkness. "Yes, you will see me again."

Will she get lossed? with severine?

< 65 >

13

Something Good to Eat

As Corinne walked through the market the next morning, she heard talk of Severine on everyone's lips.

"Did you see that woman in the green yesterday? I wonder if she will be back," said the woman with flaky skin.

"You think anyone missed a woman like that? The real question is, where is she coming back from?" said her friend, narrowing her pebble eyes. "No one seems to know anything about her." To a customer, she said, "It's fifteen for that hand of figs you've been touching up for the last five minutes." The customer sucked her teeth, *chups*, and moved on.

"When you are so pretty, everyone notices, eh?" flaky skin said.

"Everyone noticed her but nobody knows her. No one is her friend. No one is her family. Who are her people? It's very strange. Anyway, she probably won't be back today. She only seemed interested in the witch."

"But did you see the witch today?"

"Yes, her arm looks bad," said pebble eyes.

"It's a wonder she doesn't have some potions for that."

Corinne passed all the talk and spread out her cloth and arranged her oranges. She took a quick glance at the white witch, who was sitting with her eyes closed beneath her tree as though she was sleeping.

Dru's mother cleared her throat and said, "Morning, Corinne."

"Morning, Mrs. Rootsingh."

Mrs. Rootsingh darted her eyes at the witch and then back to Corinne. "You have no need of what she's selling, you hear me?" Mrs. Rootsingh said firmly.

Corinne nodded. After what had happened the day before, she wanted nothing to do with the witch. She carefully positioned herself out of the witch's line of sight. Dru peeked around her mother's sari and Corinne waved her over.

"You won't believe who came to my house yesterday," Corinne whispered.

"Who?"

"The woman in green. The same one from yesterday. Her name is Miss Severine."

Dru frowned. "Why would she go to your house?"

"My papa said she just ducked in because of the rain. I don't think she went there on purpose."

"Is your house on the main road?" Dru asked.

"No, but they were walking together from the sea."

"Did she have fish?"

"No," Corinne said.

"Who goes down to a fishing village and doesn't get some fish?" Dru asked.

Corinne shrugged. "Papa said she got there too late."

Dru's mother tucked a few long strands of hair behind her ear and cocked her head. The girls could tell she was trying to listen.

"Who is she, anyway?" Dru whispered.

"I don't know," Corinne answered quietly.

"Nobody around the market knows who she is or where she's from," Dru said.

"They can't know everyone who lives on the island, can they? I've lived here my whole life, and we never met before yesterday. And there are plenty of reasons to go to the sea besides the fish."

The girls looked up as a commotion started at one of the market entrances. Quick murmurs started up. Severine had returned. She walked directly to Corinne with a smile.

"Hello again," Severine said. She held out some coins.

Corinne wore a smug look, mainly for the benefit of pebble eyes and her friend flaky skin. "Hello, Miss Severine," she said, loud enough for everyone to hear. "Which ones would you like?"

"You pick. I know they're all very good."

Corinne made a big show of choosing her best-looking, roundest, ripest oranges. Severine wrapped them and placed them into a woven basket that was hanging from her arm. All around them, women covered their conversations behind their hands, but it was obvious whom they were talking about as their eyes darted between Severine and Corinne. Dru raised her eyebrows at Corinne, as if she was urging her to do something. Corinne understood.

"It's a beautiful day today," Corinne said. "You won't have to worry about the rain on a day like this."

"Yes, it's a nice day for a walk," Severine replied.

"Do you have a long way back to your house?"

"No, not far," Severine said.

"Then it shouldn't be any problem to get a lot of things."

"I suppose I could."

"What else will you be getting?" Corinne asked.

"I didn't manage to get any fish yesterday," Severine said. "But I think today I will have better luck." She smiled.

Dru and Corinne exchanged a quick look.

• • •

That afternoon, when Corinne got home from the market, she wasn't entirely surprised to see Severine there. But she remembered Dru's questions about the woman, and a little seed of worry planted itself in her chest.

Severine stood in the kitchen fussing over a pot. Near her, the back door hung open, and Corinne saw her father just outside cleaning some fish from a pail. Corinne sniffed at the air and made a face. "What are you doing, Miss Severine?" she asked.

"I offered to make dinner. It is the least I could do after taking up so much of your time and your father's yesterday," Severine said.

Corinne felt the worry in her chest begin to grow. But she smiled. "You shouldn't cook," she said. "You are our guest." She got between Severine and the stove and peered in.

Severine tried to gently move her aside. "I insist on it," she said. "Besides, it's the woman who does the cooking in a family."

Corinne's chest tightened at Severine's words. She leaned over the pot and inhaled its scent. It didn't smell right. It didn't smell like any food she knew. Something about the dish was off. Something about Severine was off too. Without a word, Corinne snatched up two dishcloths, grabbed the pot from the fire, and threw its contents out the back door. Severine's mouth dropped open with shock and then closed again in a straight, angry line.

70

"Hey!" Pierre jumped out of the way just in time to see the contents of the steaming pot tumble down the hill.

"That's not the way Papa likes it," Corinne said. She shook her head at Severine as if she should have known better. "I'm going to have to start all over again with a clean pot." Corinne washed out the pot, refilled it with water, and put it back on the fire. Since everything Severine had used was now sliding down to the fishing village, Corinne went to the yard to pick some vegetables and then added a few she had bought at market. "Sit. I can do this alone," she told Severine.

Pierre stepped inside briefly and hissed in Corinne's ear, "Did you have to throw out her food? It didn't smell so bad. Maybe you could have just fixed it." He made a nervous smile at Severine.

"I think you don't cook too much, Miss Severine," Corinne said. "But maybe I can show you a few things?"

"Since she started doing the cooking a year ago, she's barely let me touch the stove," Pierre added. "She thinks everyone's a terrible cook except for her. The thing is, she's probably right." He nodded his head at a chair. "Just sit and watch," he said. He went back out to the fish, but he moved close enough to the open door for Corinne to see him—and for him to see her.

Severine returned Pierre's smile and sat down. Corinne felt Severine's eyes on her as she cut the sweet potatoes and the tomatoes, chopped the cilantro, and grated the ginger. Then Corinne tossed them all into the pot and stirred.

As she cooked, the sharp, sweet smell of the ginger, tomato, and sweet potatoes rose out of the pot and filled the entire house. Corinne began to relax. She did not mind Severine looking at her as she worked. Corinne remembered the way Dru's mother watched Dru and her at the market, and she thought that was what mothers did. They watched. The worry that was growing in her began to fade.

Pierre continued to clean the fish. The snapper's reddish-silver body was limp in his hands, and the scales fell to the ground like transparent leaves as he scraped them with his knife. He cut it open and took out the bones and the guts and laid the fish flat and open for Corinne to cook. Corinne washed the fish, then filled its insides with herbs and squeezed oranges over it before she took it to the fire.

"How long ago did Corinne lose her mother, Pierre?" Severine asked.

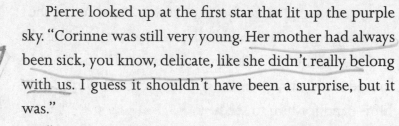

Pierre looked up at the first star that lit up the purple sky. "Corinne was still very young. Her mother had always been sick, you know, delicate, like she didn't really belong with us. I guess it shouldn't have been a surprise, but it was."

"It must have been hard to manage with such a small child and you alone."

"The other fishermen's wives were happy to take care of her when I was on the sea. And I took her out with me when I could, but Corinne has no love for the blue like me." He winked at Corinne.

"You must have been lonely yourself," Severine said.

The fish sizzled, so if Pierre answered, Corinne didn't hear it.

"I have been alone for a long time myself," Severine said. "How well does she remember her mother?"

Pierre pointed at the wax statue. "That is her mother. Exact. She remembers. I won't let her forget."

Severine turned toward Corinne. "It must be hard for you without her here." When Corinne passed near Severine to pull one of the spices out of a cupboard, Severine reached out and touched her arm.

Something about the feel of Severine's skin against her own, and the way she leaned in, probing Corinne's face, made Corinne stiffen. "Do you go to the witch often, Miss Severine?" Corinne asked.

"Corinne!" Pierre said with alarm.

Corinne looked down to avoid her father's glare, but continued anyway. "My friend Dru says that people only go to the witch to get magic for their problems."

"Corinne, stop!" Pierre said. "I'm so sorry," he said to Severine. "Why don't you step outside a minute? It's a little too hot in the kitchen."

< 73 >

Severine joined Pierre in the backyard. The two of them looked out over the ocean while Corinne watched from the open door.

"I understand why you love the sea, Pierre," Severine said. "It is beautiful." Their spot on the hill gave them a wide view of the sea, where the waves had turned orange with the final rays of the sun.

"You're right, Severine. It can be lonely on the sea," Pierre said.

"On land too," Severine replied.

Pierre and Severine looked at each other. Severine reached her hand out to Pierre.

Corinne darted to the door and yelled, "Finished!" She saw Severine pull her hand back.

"That was fast," Pierre said.

"I'm a fast cook," Corinne said.

The three had dinner by lamplight, and that night, as her father put her to bed, Corinne could see in his face that he was thinking about the evening. She remembered how the creases around his eyes deepened with pleasure when the three of them sat talking.

"It's nice having a lady around again," Pierre said.

"She's not like Mama," Corinne said.

"No. No one is like your mama. I meant that—"

"I know, Papa. I miss her too." She reached up and hugged him around his neck. She didn't know what to think about Severine, but she couldn't remember the last time her father had looked so happy. "Do you like her, Papa?"

"I think I do."

Severine made Corinne feel strange. But her papa was a good judge of people. "Then I will try to like her. For you." Still, her heart beat fast with worry.

Will Pierre and Serverine mrry eachother?

14

Cut

After market the following day, Corinne set off along-
side of Bouki, with Malik close behind and Dru last
in line. The brothers were showing off the red hills where
they lived; the ground rose sharply and the rocks were often
loose, making it just treacherous enough to keep most of
the island out. The sun had sucked away all the water from
the recent rain. There was hardly anything wet on the island. Even the leaves on the trees hung limp. The boys shot
down a couple of juicy pomeracs to help with their thirst.

They crunched through the bright pink pomerac skin
to the sweet, white flesh inside, tossing the big round
seeds behind them as they walked. After about four, Bouki

spoke up. "How do you like your new mother, Corinne? She's visited your house two days in a row. If she's there again tonight, watch out. She's going to take over."

Corinne wiped her mouth against her sleeve. "She's not my mother. I run my own house," she said.

Malik began to snicker.

Bouki answered, "Not for long you don't. Now if she were ugly, you'd stand a chance." He tossed a seed and pulled another pomerac out of his pocket.

"My father doesn't need her," Corinne said.

"Oh, *sure,* he doesn't *need* her. Who needs a woman, eh brother? Especially a pretty one."

"She is pretty." Dru nodded. "I heard my mother say so too. She called her beauty 'rare.'"

Malik pointed to the sky and dove his finger down.

Bouki said, "My brother thinks you should be extra careful with this one since she just dropped out of the sky."

Corinne sighed. "How do you know that a lady won't scoop up the two of you one day? You could get a mother, too, you know."

"I've told you before," Bouki said. "We don't need a mother."

"Even a pretty one?" Corinne teased.

"Least of all one of those. The pretty ones are bad business."

"Not all the pretty ones!" Dru said. "But that Severine appeared out of nowhere. Don't you think it's strange?

Why doesn't your father think so? And how come she isn't in her own house making her own dinner?"

The troubling little feeling in Corinne's chest grew again, but she held her chin up. "My papa doesn't think it's strange. He knows what he's doing."

"The adults are always pairing up. It's truly sad," Bouki said with a shake of his head.

Corinne turned on him. "My mama and papa were together all the time. They weren't sad a day in their lives when she was ... before she ... well, they were never sad."

"And my parents are together all the time too," Dru added. "They don't look sad either. What's so wrong with pairing off?"

"Who wants to be with the same person all the time?" Bouki asked.

Malik snorted and nodded in agreement.

"Maybe nobody wants to pair up with the likes of you, Bouki," Corinne said.

Malik grinned.

"Ho. Ho. You two are comic." Bouki grabbed the end of Corinne's shirt and tried to pull her off-balance, but Corinne twisted around and pulled away from his grip. He ran before she could give him a shove.

"You're all by yourself, and you're slow!" she called, tossing her pomerac seed and dashing off after him.

Bouki and Corinne ran to the top of a high rocky ridge. Bouki ran nimbly over the uneven surface. But Corinne was determined to beat him at his game. She was close behind. Suddenly, Bouki stopped.

"See that?" he asked.

"Don't try to trick me," Corinne said. She was nearly on him now.

"No, look." He pointed into the valley at the white witch bent over what looked like a small iron pot.

"What is she doing?" Corinne asked, stopping beside him and catching her breath.

"I don't want to find out," Bouki said. He narrowed his eyes and began to back away slowly. "They say she can turn people into animals."

"That's ridiculous."

"They say she's more than two hundred years old."

"Impossible!" Corinne said with a laugh. Her laugh echoed around the valley, and the witch looked around, trying to pinpoint where it had come from.

Bouki dropped to the ground. "You'd better hide," he whispered.

At first, Corinne didn't budge. But when the white witch began to turn in their direction, Corinne remembered that day at the river when the witch had called her stupid and told her to go home to her mother. A strange, cold feeling came over her. She dropped to the ground. As she fell, a sharp rock sliced her leg open, and Corinne screamed as pain shot through her.

Bouki scrambled over to Corinne and put a dirt-and

pomerac-stained hand over her mouth to muffle the sound. Once she stopped, he helped her back down the hill.

Dru gasped. "That looks awful!" she said.

Corinne looked at the blood covering her leg. "It's not so bad," she said in a brave voice. But when she tried to walk without Bouki's help, a jolt of pain made her cry out and fall again.

Malik pulled off his brother's cloth belt to bandage the deep gash. Corinne would have protested at the dirty cloth, but words wouldn't form in her mouth. With the cloth tied securely around her leg, Bouki and Dru ducked their heads under Corinne's arms and hoisted her up. They were going to carry her home.

It was after dark when they arrived. Every step hurt Corinne more and more. She felt weak and cold. As soon as they reached the path to Corinne's house, her papa burst through the front door. He scooped up Corinne and took her inside. Dru and the boys followed to explain what had happened.

Dru untied the piece of cloth that was around Corinne's wound. She tried to hand it back to Bouki, but he held his palm up and turned his face away. Dru sighed. "I told them that running around the island was dangerous, but they would never listen to me."

Pierre nodded. "Thanks for bringing her home. Just lie back, Corinne. I'm going to go get some water to wash the cut."

Corinne lay back against the couch, while Pierre hurried from the room.

That was when Severine stepped toward them. "Let me take a look," she said.

Corinne had not noticed Severine was there. As Severine came forward, Corinne's muscles tightened. Dru and the brothers took a step back, looking at each other with wary eyes, but Corinne had nowhere to go.

"So delicate," Severine said softly. She put her finger into Corinne's cut, and Corinne howled in pain.

Malik ran between Severine and Corinne and stood stiff like a guard.

"What are you doing?" Dru asked the woman.

Severine leveled an angry stare at the four of them just as Corinne's father returned with a clean, wet cloth. Malik moved out of the way, but Severine stood her ground.

"Step aside, Severine," Pierre said.

"I know what to do to help," Severine insisted. She put her palm on the cut and muttered something under her breath.

Corinne thought she saw Severine's eyes flash with yellow light. She screamed again.

"You're hurting her!" Pierre pushed Severine aside. She stumbled backward as Pierre began to gently wash Corinne's cut.

Corinne winced in pain again, and her eyes squeezed shut. "Papa," she whispered.

She felt her father's cool fingers brush against her hot skin. "Shh," Pierre said softly. "I'm here. You know I'll always take care of you. It'll be over soon."

Severine's face was hard. She put her hand on Pierre's shoulder. "You don't know what you're doing," she told him. "I know what will help her."

He shook her off. "I can take care of my own daughter, Severine."

Severine's eyes burned with anger until they shone like hot coals. While Pierre finished tending to Corinne, Severine looked around as if she didn't know what to do next. Her eyes stopped on an object across the room. Corinne saw that she had found her mother's wax statue. She gasped.

Pierre picked up the cloth he had pressed against Corinne's leg. "Sorry, sorry," he said. "I'll be more gentle."

Severine stomped to the shelf and picked up the hard wax figure in her hands. She looked at Corinne with her eyes hard and shining and dropped it on the floor. The wax broke into two pieces that skidded in opposite directions.

Severine stormed out into the night. Corinne looked at Malik and pointed at the open door. Malik nodded once, and headed toward it, waving for his brother and Dru to follow. Dru picked up the statue pieces and wrapped them in the end of her sari. Dru peered back into the room where Pierre still leaned over Corinne with an apologetic smile, then Dru rushed after the brothers into the night.

Corinne winced as her father wrapped her cut, but she kept trying to see out the door.

"Stop moving, Corinne," Pierre said. "You're making it worse." He went out to the back to wash out the cloths in a bucket.

Corinne tried to lie still and listen, but there was nothing except the usual sounds of animals in the night. Then came the sound of footsteps running up the path.

"She's gone," Bouki said.

"Where?" Corinne asked.

"We lost sight of her around a bend. When we got there—"

"She had disappeared," Dru finished.

Malik spread his fingers wide and moved his hands apart to look like something blowing away with the wind.

"That's not possible," Corinne said.

"We looked everywhere," Dru said. She ducked her head and lowered her voice when Pierre walked back into the room. "She wasn't up or down the road."

"Malik looked on the ground for tracks, but he could not find any," Bouki said.

"Where could she have gone?" Corinne asked. But an idea was already starting to form, and her heart began to beat faster.

Malik turned toward the window and pointed out at the trees.

"Nobody would go in that forest," Dru said. "Especially not at night."

"Unless Severine is no body," Bouki whispered.

Dru pulled her braid through her fingers and tugged at the end. "No, she can't be," she said. "Their kind can't come out during the day. The light destroys them."

"But what else can she be?" Corinne said. "I didn't believe in them before, but maybe she really is a—"

"Don't say it," Dru pleaded, but the word was already on Corinne's lips.

"*Jumbie.*"

What will they
Put in the Potion

15

Muddy Tears

The jumbie crawled with ease over thick trunks and gnarled underbrush, even though night in the forest was pitch-black. After centuries of moving among these trees, she knew the paths through the dark and tangled roots as if she had carved them out herself. The branches that caught at the hair of humans and the picker bushes that scratched their skin never hurt her. She knew each one. She also knew when people had walked through them. She could smell their blood on the edges of thorns and the scent of their skin on even the tiniest thread that got ripped off of their clothing. In this forest, the ground, and every plant that grew from it, made way for the jumbie. But people didn't have her command. Plus, they were clumsy and afraid, and the creatures in the mahogany forest happily made obstacles for them if they dared to pass through.

Usually, the farther she walked into her own land, the happier she became, but not on this night. On this night all she could think about was the way Pierre dismissed her, how he pushed her aside. The night before had been so different. She thought she was gaining their trust. But now everything had changed.

"They don't see me as family," the jumbie muttered. "They only see each other." She seethed. "They will never accept me." A muddy tear spilled onto her cheek, then sprouted legs and crawled down her body. "I was right all along. This island was better before people came to it. It is time for them to go. But not before I repay their kind for luring my sister away from me."

The jumbie's hand shot out and grabbed a small furry creature by the neck. It wriggled as Severine squeezed tighter and tighter with her thumb and forefinger until the small bones snapped and the creature became still. She brought the dead animal to her chest and stroked it. "I will give my sister's child a choice. Maybe she can be convinced to join me." She squeezed the animal again, and for a moment, it trembled as if it was coming back to life, but it was only a flicker. She opened her mouth and gobbled the little creature, bones, fur, and all. "I can feel the power in her," the jumbie said after she swallowed the animal's crunched-up bones. She licked her lips. "And I need it."

the jumbie will capkcher. corinne

16

Little Men

In the morning, Corinne unwrapped her father's bandage and found a soft red scab covering her wound. She touched it. It hurt, but not too much.

She picked her oranges for the day and walked slowly to market. As she limped up the dusty road, the forest on her right side seemed to crowd in. She began to sweat, and the hairs on her arms stood on end. For the first time, the mahogany forest made her heart beat hard inside her chest. She remembered the eyes she had seen in the forest days ago, and she remembered that last night, Severine's eyes had the same gleam.

It's the same forest I've lived next to every day of my

life, she told herself as the shiver crawled up her arms like a wave of insects. *The stories about jumbies are just things that grown people say when they make up stories at night.* She tried to laugh off the idea of Severine as a jumbie. She walked on a few steps. *But what did those eyes belong to? And where did Severine come from? She said she lived close enough to walk, but no one knows her.*

Corinne put down her basket near the well and slipped a few of the small oranges into her pockets. She hesitated for a moment but thought of her father and the way he looked at Severine last night, like she was a stranger. Corinne crossed the road, pushed aside a tangle of branches, and stepped inside the forest.

It was cooler among the trees. A few harmless animals scurried away from her feet. She swallowed hard and moved on. When the road was out of sight, she put an orange in the crook of a branch to mark the spot where she entered. She walked on for a few minutes, searched around, and placed oranges as markers, but she found nothing that seemed out of place for a forest. Then, on the other side of a tree, she heard a light rustle. Her pulse quickened. She followed the sound and placed her last orange in a branch above her. Around the other side of the tree trunk, a shrub shivered as though something had just gone past it. She followed the shaking path of leaves until they stopped beneath a fat, short tree. She combed the leaves apart and looked behind them.

"Oh!" Corinne said, surprised.

There was a child sitting on the damp ground, playing with soft, wet dirt between its fingers. It was wearing a woven straw hat shaped like a short, wide cone.

When the child looked up at her, beneath the hat brim Corinne could only see its mouth. It was shaped into the form of an *O*. It echoed. "Oh. Oh, oh, oh. Oh!" And with each syllable, the voice grew deeper until it was less like a child's and more like a man's.

Corinne stepped back. She saw several other little man-children standing around the squat tree. The small thing had not been imitating her. It had been calling to its own kind. Corinne had heard enough stories to know that these could be *douens*—baby spirits that steal children straight from their homes.

Corinne froze with fear. There was something else she had heard about douens. As one of the little men got up, Corinne tried to see its feet. It took an awkward step toward her. Its feet were turned backward. Now she was sure. A scream left Corinne's throat. A small flock of kiskadees rose up into the air, and a *manicou* and a bright green iguana scurried into some underbrush. The sound of the animals moving unfroze Corinne and she ran too.

Corinne went to the last tree she'd marked and grabbed the orange. She turned and threw it at the little jumbie coming toward her. The jumbie caught it and continued on. Corinne ran to the next tree. Now all the douens were

< 90 >

moving toward her. With every step, they chanted, "Oh, oh, oh!" The sound filled her ears, her head, and matched time with her heartbeat until it felt like the douens' sounds were becoming part of her. It took all her strength to grab the next orange and throw again. This one burst on the shoulder of another douen, but the tough little jumbie walked on as if nothing had touched it.

Corinne kept moving, though each step felt harder than the last, like swimming against a current. She threw a third orange as hard as she could behind her. Then there were no more oranges. She looked for the road, but it was nowhere near. She had marked more trees, she was sure of it, but the oranges were all gone. She was lost.

Her heart pounded faster. She looked around for a clue of which way to run, but all the trees looked alike. She tried to feel the air against her cheek, but all she noticed was sweat dripping down her skin. Her legs felt weak and wobbly. She couldn't get them to move the way she wanted to. The douens had her surrounded.

The army of tiny douens was closing in, their calls growing louder and louder, when a small frog hopped into the circle and stopped in front of Corinne.

"Oh," the douens said, distracted by the frog. "Oh, oh, oh."

It hopped once toward them. The douen closest to the frog leaned in. A few licked their lips. Just as one of the douens lunged at it, the frog hopped out of reach.

It hopped closer to the douens again, and hopped away when another one of them tried to grab it. Each time, the frog drew them farther and farther away from Corinne.

Was that the same frog from the well? Corinne barely had time to wonder as the frog lured the douens all together. When they all lunged for the frog, the jumbies landed in a heap, some with their fingers just a hair's breadth from the frog's back legs. The frog turned and hopped toward a barely noticeable path. Then it turned again and hopped away deeper into the forest. Without the douens' sounds filling her head, Corinne could think clearly. Her legs began to work again. She sprinted down the path the frog had revealed. Her injured leg hurt, but she didn't stop.

A few moments later, she burst out onto the road and stood panting and blinking in the sunlight.

Dru was right. Jumbies are real.

Where does the trail lead

17

The Jumbies

Dru held her sari up over her knees as she ran hard toward the well. She spotted Corinne and stopped herself by grabbing on to Corinne's shoulders. The girls held on tight to each other until they found enough breath to speak.

"I'm sorry I didn't believe you about the jumbies," Corinne said. She pointed to the forest. "There are douens in there!"

Dru held Corinne's hand. "I got away from Mami as early as I could. What about Miss Severine? Did she come back?"

Corinne's legs felt like they might fail her again. She shook her head no.

< 93 >

"If she went into the forest last night like we thought, and there are douens in there, then we're sure she can only be one of them too."

"I know," Corinne said. "But she is not like the little men, the douens."

"No. My mother said she must be a La Diabless. A devil-woman," Dru said. "Have you ever seen Miss Severine's feet? She always wears that long dress."

Corinne frowned. "What do you mean?"

"La Diabless are always beautiful women, but they have one cow hoof instead of a foot," Dru explained. "They lure men into the forest and kill them."

Even with the long dress, Corinne was sure she would have noticed if Severine walked with one cow hoof. "No. Not a La Diabless." Corinne knew her father was safe on the sea that morning. "If she was, she would have killed my father the first night. What else could she be?"

"Whatever she is, you have to stay away from her," Dru pleaded. "Our kind and their kind don't belong together."

"But she keeps coming to us," Corinne said.

"Tell your father to lock the doors."

Corinne knew that her father did not believe in jumbies, and he would not believe Severine was one. There was only one person Corinne thought could help them, even though she got a cold feeling at the thought of her. "What about the white witch? She knows magic."

For a moment, both girls hesitated.

Corinne picked up the basket that she had left on the road and looked toward the market. "The faster we get this over with, the faster everything will be the way it was," Corinne said, as a way to coax them both.

The girls held hands and headed off.

• • •

The witch made a long sigh when Corinne arrived in front of her blanket. "Are you in trouble again?" she asked without looking up. She handed a paper-wrapped package to her customer and dropped the coins he paid into her pouch with three loud clinks.

Corinne stepped closer. "Tell me about Miss Severine, the woman in green."

The man, who was just leaving, stopped dead in his tracks and looked from the witch to Corinne and back again. The white witch rubbed her withered left arm and cut him an evil look. "Why don't you mind your own business?" she snapped and he scurried away. She turned back to Corinne. "Is that what she is calling herself? Well, I am not getting involved with her. And I advise that you do the same."

"I can't do that now. It's too late," Corinne said. "You have to do something to help me."

"Do I?" the witch grumbled. She touched her arm again.

"We think she's a jumbie that lives in the forest. We think she might be dangerous," Corinne said.

"We?" The witch looked behind Corinne and saw Dru hovering at a distance, twirling a long braid around her finger. "Well, I think swimming in rivers when no one knows where you are and running off into the forest alone is dangerous. I think you like to look for dangerous things."

Corinne was startled. How had the witch known about her running into the forest alone? "I didn't go looking for Severine," Corinne said. Her voice dropped low. "But I think she might have come looking for me."

"What would she want with a scrawny little thing like you?"

"I don't know. I only need to know how to get rid of her."

The witch laughed. "Impossible. The jumbies have lived on this island long before people were even dreamt of. She won't go away so easily."

"So she is a jumbie then?" Dru said as she took a single step forward.

"Hush!" the witch hissed.

"Our kind and their kind don't belong together," Corinne said with a nod to Dru.

"Our kind? What do you know about our kind and their kind, little one? You can't even tell the difference. You are new to this world. Trust in those who have been around much, much longer than you." The witch moved around a few things on her blanket. "You must accept that things are the way they are for a reason. Here's my advice: The next time you see this Severine coming, go the other way."

"But she comes to my house," Corinne said.

The witch's eyebrows twitched as she searched Corinne's face. "Then you're right. It is too late." The witch's shoulders drooped. Her left arm dangled useless at her side. "There is no hope for you. She is a bad one."

"But you have to do something!" Dru shrieked. She now stood by Corinne's side.

The witch avoided the girls' stares as she shook her head. Her sparse white braids tossed. "I'm sorry. There is nothing I can do."

"Then I'll have to take care of her myself." Corinne turned.

"Corinne, wait!" Dru grabbed her arm. "What are you going to do by yourself? That will only be trouble."

Corinne pulled her arm away. "This time, I didn't trouble trouble. Trouble came troubling me. And I intend to do something about it." She turned toward the road.

"You must pay me for my time!" the witch yelled.

Dru took an orange from Corinne's basket and threw it at the old woman. The witch made a deft catch with her good hand. Her long yellow nails clicked together around the fruit. Corinne and Dru both shuddered at the sound. Then Corinne ran to the sea.

By the time Corinne got to the shore, her cut had

ripped open again and her leg was shining with blood, but she barely noticed. She needed to find her father. She skidded to a halt. Corinne's chest felt tight and her breath came in hard, painful bursts. His yellow boat lay in the sand, empty. The nets were dry and neatly gathered in the prow of the boat, the way they were every morning before he cast off.

His boat had never left the shore.

Pierre is with
Seurienne and I
think she will
kill Pierre.

18

The Stew

Back at Corinne's house, Severine stood over the stove, stirring something in a large pot.

"It smells terrific," Pierre said. "I'm glad you came. I've never seen the sky as bad as it was today." He looked out of the window and shook his head, though the sky was perfectly clear.

Severine looked over at him with a wicked smile. The magic she had used to cloud his vision had worked perfectly. Where everyone on the island saw clear blue sky, Pierre saw a raging storm. Now she only needed to finish cooking up her last bit of magic to have complete control over his thoughts. She hummed and stirred. Just like

Corinne, Severine had put in grated ginger and chopped cilantro. She needed to change the smell just enough to fool Pierre.

"This is the worst storm I've ever seen," Pierre continued. "Imagine if I had taken out the boat." He sighed. "If Corinne was left alone in this world . . ."

"The sea couldn't take you if it tried," Severine said in a syrupy sweet voice. "I'm only glad I saw you this morning and could keep you company. If I hadn't, you would be home alone all day."

"Corinne should have come right back home," Pierre said. "She can't be safe in these winds."

"I told you, I saw her with that girl with the long braids. The girl's mother took her with them."

"That's the nice thing about having a mother," Pierre said softly. "Someone is always there to take care of you."

"Yes, a family is a nice thing, isn't it?" Severine reached into a fold of her skirt and took out an old gnarled plant root, covered in white fungus. She dropped it into the pot and stirred again. She continued to hum something low and lilting to make Pierre feel sleepy.

She ladled the stew into a bowl and put it in front of Pierre. Then she stood over him and waited for him to taste the magic and give up his mind to her. Pierre picked up the spoon and inhaled.

"Wonderful!" he said. He lifted the spoon to his lips.

Severine leaned in to make sure every single drop went

in. She watched him intently as the liquid went down his throat, and something in his eyes began to change. They became cloudy, as if a storm was swirling right in his eyes. She watched Pierre scoop more of the stew into his mouth. Then he dropped the spoon and attacked the bowl like a greedy animal. When it was empty, he tipped it up to get every last bit onto his tongue. Severine's smile grew. Pierre held out the bowl to Severine for a second helping, just as Corinne opened the front door.

I think corinne will be like her dad.

19

The Storm

Corinne breathed in the foul smell that was coming from the kitchen. It made her stomach turn and her eyes water. She put one hand over her nose and rushed inside. The windows had all been shut and Severine stood in the shadows, watching Pierre eat.

Corinne knocked the bowl off the table and pulled the spoon away from her father. "Papa, don't eat that!" she said. Her father did not respond.

Severine stepped into a shaft of light. "Where have you been?" she asked with a smirk. "I made lunch for us." She held out another bowl to Corinne.

Corinne slapped it out of her hand.

Severine's eyes narrowed, but her lips curled into a cruel arch.

"Papa!" Corinne called. She touched her father's hand. He looked up at her, but he didn't seem to recognize her. "Papa?" Tears covered her face as she shook him, called to him, and tried to make him answer her.

"Why don't you have some stew?" Severine asked. She picked up the bowl from the ground and ladled in some more of the foul-smelling slop.

"Get out of my house!" Corinne screamed.

"*Your* house?"

"Yes. *My* house." She pulled aside curtains from the kitchen window and pushed the window open to let out the smell.

Light streamed in and fell directly on Pierre's face, but he didn't even blink. The magic that Severine had put in his eyes blinded him to anything but the visions she had created.

Severine walked in a circle around the table. Corinne backed away, trying to keep the table between them. In the sunlight, Severine's body seemed different. She looked thinner and a bit hairy.

"Papa? Please help!"

"Oh Papa! Help!" Severine mocked. "He can't see you. He can only see the darkness and a wild storm outside. That storm is so terrible, I'm afraid it could kill you. Which is what I will tell him happened to you if you don't behave yourself. Better to have him think you were killed by a storm instead of me, don't you think?" Severine laughed. "He can't help you at all. So who will protect you now?"

Corinne backed away more. She felt the fear rush through her body, making every movement feel clumsy. A whimper escaped from her throat.

Severine stepped closer. "Stop that ridiculous whining."

Corinne felt anger flare up inside her and temporarily held the fear in check. She threw Severine a heated stare. Severine pushed the bowl of stew toward Corinne. Corinne jerked away, causing Severine to slop stew onto the floor. Severine grabbed Corinne's wrist and shoved her to the ground, right into the foul-smelling stew. "You can't resist me!" Severine shrieked.

The stew felt like it was burning into Corinne's skin. She got up quickly. "Leave us alone!" she screamed as she wiped herself off.

When Corinne looked up, she saw that Severine's face had narrowed, her nose and mouth protruded slightly like an animal's, and her arms looked as brittle and thin as sticks.

"Are you going to make me leave?" Severine asked, straight in Corinne's face.

Corinne wanted to fight, but found herself stepping back yet again. She moved into a sliver of light and the sun caught on the stone pendant around her neck.

Severine stared at the necklace, and her mouth slackened

as if surprised. In that moment of hesitation, Corinne saw her chance. She threw her body at Severine, hoping to knock her down. But Severine only staggered back against the stove and grabbed hold of the stew pot. "You can't stop me," she said and threw the hot stew on Corinne.

Corinne's skin burned. She ran outside to the back of the house. She threw a bucket of rainwater over her head. The magic still felt like flames.

She ran down the hill to the sea and dove into the waves. The water rolled and tumbled her against the grainy bottom. It burned the gash on her leg, but at last the rest of her skin began to cool. She floated on the waves, letting them move her back and forth a few feet from the shore until the burning stopped. She saw her house up on the hill and Severine standing at the kitchen door with a look of satisfaction. For a moment, Corinne thought she saw Severine's eyes flash yellow again.

Severine was in Corinne's house. She had Corinne's father. Corinne called to her grand-père in the ocean and her mama in heaven for help, but there was no answer, only the sound of the waves as they broke against the sand, saying, "Hush, hush, hush."

— Will she get bit by a shark?

20

One Bite

The white witch hobbled into her little hut on the mud island at the center of the swamp. She dropped her considerable weight on the only bench in the room and sighed. She rubbed her withered arm and then reached down to massage her tired legs. From her bags, she fished out the perfectly round orange Dru had tossed to her that morning as payment. She pierced the skin with one long, yellow fingernail, and peeled the orange, savoring the smell that burst out of its skin. It was a beautiful thing—bright, pungent, and resilient. She broke it into segments and breathed in its sweetness. As soon as she popped the first piece into her mouth, and the juice burst into her puckered, aged cheeks, her eyes flashed with surprise. Immediately, she knew three things:

1. No ordinary child could have grown such extraordinary fruit.
2. Severine would want the child for her own.
3. To protect the child required magic that was far beyond the witch's own abilities.

The witch looked at the orange in her hand and wondered aloud, "Why would Nicole have hidden her true self from me?"

Is nicholen corinnes mom? What type of jumbie was she?

21

The Cave

Corinne was lying in her father's boat with a small crowd of children standing around it when Bouki and Malik found her at the end of the day. Her friend Laurent was arguing with Victor, one of the fishermen, but their conversations moved in and out of her consciousness as if they were waves.

"It's her father's boat," Laurent said. "She can stay in it if she wants."

"Her father would not want her in there," Victor said gruffly. "It's not a place for children to play."

Corinne became aware of the smell of food cooking that mingled with the scent of the salty sea.

"I will come back later to check the boats," Victor continued. "And if she's still there I will take her out myself. Now, it looks like your suppers are ready, and your bathwater is getting cold. It's time for all you children to go home."

One by one, Corinne heard their footsteps slapping against the wet sand as they left. She heard the old fisherman sigh before he left, then she lay quietly among her father's nets, with only Bouki and Malik watching over her. The boys climbed in. Malik rubbed the evening chill from his arms.

"You can come and stay with us tonight if you want," Bouki offered. "Dru is probably already at home tucked in beside her mother." He grinned at Corinne as if he was willing her to join him.

Corinne pretended not to hear. She looked up at her house on the hill. In one of the windows, there was the glow of a light. *What was her papa doing right at that moment? Could he be cured? How was she going to get Severine out?* She felt so tired.

Malik stood up and grabbed one of Corinne's arms. He started to pull her up. Bouki joined him. Between them, the boys managed to drag Corinne out of the boat. She followed them toward town, not thinking of where she was going, not seeing the road before her, only seeing Severine's animal face and the yellow light flashing from her eyes. If only she had stayed away from the forest in the first place. Then Severine would have never come to them. Her father would be safe. All the years her papa had protected her, and now she could not do the same for him. Her chest burned with grief.

Corinne pretended not to see the look of worry in the brothers' eyes as they looked at each other. She concentrated on making her legs move away from her house as they walked inland under the brightening stars, away from the arc of purple that outlined the sea.

"It's dinnertime," Bouki said as they came to the main road that led into town. He tried to sound cheerful, but it came out too high-pitched, like a cricket chirping.

"Not for us," Corinne muttered.

"And why not? Everybody's got to eat something," Bouki said in his regular voice. He smiled and nudged his brother. "We'll show you how to get dinner when you're on your own."

Malik walked ahead and beckoned for Corinne to follow him. He led them into the center of town. They zigzagged through small footpaths and behind houses so they would not be seen in the light of the lamps that hung over the stone roads. When they got to the bakery, they stopped and breathed in the fresh baked goods from the oven. There was one lamp inside, hanging over the counter. Nearly all the shelves were bare.

Through one small window, the children saw the baker. Corinne had not seen him since the night at the graveyard when all the trouble began. Hugo was big enough to knead stone into bread, but his large arms laid out a pair of delicate pastries on a counter and covered them gently with a white cloth. Corinne and the boys watched him close up the cupboards and sweep the floors. Then he disappeared into the back.

Malik dashed in, faster than Corinne had ever seen him move. He lifted the cloth and grabbed the pastries, then dashed back out as soundlessly as a specter. He held them out. Bouki divided what they had between the three of them and led the group away.

• • •

Bouki and Malik lived in a cave that was in the middle of the red hills, facing away from the sea, and sheltered from the easterly wind. The rock and smooth floor of the cave was reddish brown. When the brothers leaned against the rocks to finish eating, Corinne noticed that their skin and hair was the same red color as their home. Standing still, they looked like statues carved out of the rocks around them, with their hair like kinky mud spirals that pointed in every direction.

Toward the back of the cave were a few scraps of cloth where the brothers slept, and in the middle was a circle of rocks where they made their fire to keep warm at night, or to cook anything that may have fallen into their hands during the day.

Malik brought one of the cloths and draped it over Corinne's shoulders.

"You can stay for as long as you like," Bouki said. "Just don't try to mother us."

Corinne nodded.

That night, she discovered that the cave was cozy and warm, and that the blankets the brothers had loaned her were quite soft. But even so, she wasn't able to sleep well. She kept thinking of her father, sitting in the kitchen, looking lost inside his own skin. And Severine's cruel laugh echoed all around her.

In the morning, when the brothers woke up, she was sitting at the mouth of the cave, fingering her stone necklace.

"Breakfast?" Bouki asked. Without waiting, he walked away. Corinne thought he was going to steal from the baker again, but when he returned, he had three coconuts, some bananas, and a long stalk of sugarcane. Bouki drew out a knife from the back of his pants, cut the sugarcane stalk into three pieces, and divided it among them. They sucked the cane in silence. Corinne barely noticed the sweet stalks, was barely even aware of her own movement when she picked out the sugarcane strings that got caught in her teeth. After the cane, Bouki hacked off the tops of the coconuts and they each put one to their mouths to drink the cool water inside. Then he cut the coconuts in half and sliced off a sliver from each husk for scooping out the soft jelly. When they were done with those, Malik passed out the bananas.

With food in her stomach, Corinne felt stronger and more confident. "I have to get back to my house," she told Bouki and Malik. "I have to get her away from my papa." She stood up and started toward her house. Malik ran ahead of her. He shook his head and waved his hands to get her to stop.

"You couldn't do it yesterday," Bouki pointed out. "Why do you think it will be different now?"

"I have to do something," Corinne said. "I'm going now."

She stepped forward, but Malik blocked her way and crossed his arms across his chest.

"We can't let you do that," Bouki said. "Not without knowing what to do first. Dru seems to know about these jumbies. We'll ask her."

Corinne thought for a moment, and then nodded. She let the brothers lead her toward Dru's village. But it was all taking too long.

She lagged behind them. Then, in a thicket of trees, she doubled back quietly and burst into a run toward her own house.

She had to get back to her father.

22

Family

When Corinne got to her front yard, she picked up a dry branch from the ground and held it over her head like a weapon. She pushed through the door and went straight to her father. He was still sitting in a chair in the kitchen. He looked very old, as if a layer of gray had settled on him overnight. Even his eyes were clouded and waxy like a blind man's. Severine was nowhere to be seen.

Corinne dropped the branch and ran back outside. She picked an orange and went back in to slice it open and squeeze some of the juice onto her father's parched lips. His tongue flicked out and licked some of it. As soon as he did, the clouds began to part from his eyes. Corinne gave him some more. Pierre's eyes darted around the room. Finally, they settled on his daughter.

"Corinne?"

"Yes, Papa," Corinne said, relieved.

His eyes were soft, like she had always known them to be, but in an instant, they turned hard with fear. "Corinne, run!"

Corinne jumped out of the way just as a heavy wooden rolling pin crashed down on the arm of the chair, right where she had been just a moment before. Pieces of the chair splintered onto the floor. Corinne grabbed for her branch, but Severine kicked it away. Corinne looked back to her father, but the clouds over his eyes had returned. He saw nothing.

Even though Severine stood in the shadows, there was enough light coming through one of the windows so that Corinne could see her even more clearly than she had the day before. Severine's skin looked dry and shriveled, like old tree bark under a layer of downy brown hair. She had grown thin and so long that she had to hunch so she wouldn't hit the ceiling. Her eyes were huge in her gaunt face and shining with yellow light. Now the green cloth that covered her body barely reached her knees and hung in gaping panels. Two thin legs with bare feet and toes like scraggly roots stretched out beneath her. Severine was not a La Diabless. Only Corinne didn't know what other jumbie she could be.

"I was wondering how long it would take you to come back," Severine said. "You must have missed me. But now I'm not sure I want you around pestering me anymore. You're a lot of trouble."

"When you trouble trouble, trouble comes troubling you," Corinne said. "And you came to us!"

"Ah, ah, ah!" Severine shook a finger at Corinne. "What you don't know, little girl, could fill up the entire ocean. I was here first. This is my island. People came to me, sailing on the ocean in ships filled to the brim with people. I destroyed all the ships and I should have made sure that all of you drowned in the sea, but I was stupid. I allowed too many of you to swim to shore. That was a mistake."

As Severine moved around the room, she carefully avoided the few shafts of light that came through the window. Corinne felt fear flare up in her again and eyed the big iron skillet on the counter. She began to inch toward it. She hoped that Severine would not notice. "Why did you let them come then?" Corinne asked, her voice trembling. "If you didn't want them to live here, why did you allow it?" She moved steadily along the counter as she spoke.

"I had a sister. She pitied people. She went inside the ships and saw that some of the people were chained below. She helped them escape and swim to the island while I dealt with the others. If I had seen what she was doing, I would have stopped her."

"Chains?"

"Yes. Didn't you know that?" Severine laughed. "Is there anything you do know? Some of the people chained up others and left them to rot in the bottoms of their ships. My sister felt sorry for them. I never did."

"You are a terrible—" Corinne struggled to find a word to describe the creature in front of her.

"You know what I am. Say it! Say what they call me."

"Jumbie!"

"Yes. That's it. I didn't like pretending to be human, but my sister did. She pretended often so she could spend time with people. Then she must have started to believe she was human because she did the most stupid human thing of all. She fell in love—with your father." Severine's eyes pierced Corinne.

Corinne's muscles went slack. She stood motionless just a few inches from the skillet. It couldn't be true. She looked at her papa, at Severine, at the house her mama had helped to make. Her throat was dry. She couldn't speak.

"I should have known not to let—what did your kind call her—*Nicole* go among people," Severine was saying. "They are infectious little parasites and she was too good for them. She lowered herself to be with the likes of your father and then what happened to her? Where is she now?"

Corinne found her voice. It was raspy and soft. "What are you talking about?"

< 117 >

Severine crouched down so that her eyes were at the same level as Corinne's. "Your mother lied to your father about who she really was. At first I thought her pretending was a good thing. She would lie to the humans, gain their trust, perhaps recruit some of them to our side. But all she stole was his heart and, in the end, *he* stole *her* life. That is why it's better to be who you are. Better to stay with your own kind." Severine looked Corinne up and down. "If you know who your own kind is." She smiled. It was almost gentle. "I thought I had lost my family. But look, here we all are together at last."

"You are a liar! I am no family of yours." Corinne reached behind her and found the handle of the skillet. She raised it over her head and grunted as she pelted it toward the jumbie.

Severine caught it easily and put it down on the table. She shook her head. "Is that any way to treat your auntie?" she asked.

"Stop saying that! You are not my family!" Corinne screamed.

"No? I am your mother's sister—your precious mother who loved you so much that she chose to give up her own life. Yes, that is what living among humans does to us. It kills us," Severine said.

"She didn't. She didn't choose to leave us. She was sick. Papa said so. She would never—"

"Your precious papa had no idea who his wife was.

Did you Pierre?" Severine moved over to him and shook his head for him. "No? There. That's straight from the jumbie's mouth."

"My papa is not a jumbie."

Severine looked at Pierre. "Not yet," she said. "But soon he will be."

Corinne rammed into Severine, clawing and slapping and kicking her as hard as she could. Severine held out one long twiggy hand and easily held Corinne away from her body. She laughed again. "You are more like me than you think, little girl. So I'm going to give you a chance to join your real family. Your father is already on our side. You can come too.

"You must have known that you were better than the other children," Severine said. "Who among them can climb trees as quickly as you? Who among them could chase an animal into the forest and catch it? Who among them could see a jumbie looking at them from the shadows of the forest and make it out alive? You are part of this island. That is why you are so comfortable on it." Severine pulled herself up to her full height. Her head bumped the ceiling. She stretched out. Her arms and face hardened like tree bark. The hair on her skin bristled. Severine's eyes flashed with anger, and Corinne noticed that the shape of them was so similar to her mother's.

Corinne felt numb. Her hand went up to her necklace and she fingered the stone's smooth face.

"I was the one you saw that day in the forest," Severine said. "I followed you out. Then you and your father led me to my very own sister. Thank you for that. I might never have found her. And I had no idea that you even existed." She stepped forward and grabbed Corinne's chin in her dry, rough hand. Corinne tried to pull away, but Severine's grip grew tighter. "Now I know I can live in the world with people. She found the way. But she was weak. I am stronger. I can take my time to turn all the people on the island. I can make this island what it once was. We can all be one kind. One family."

Corinne squirmed under Severine's hand and felt sick to her stomach at the thought of an island filled with jumbies. She reached behind her again, looking for something else to protect her, but there was nothing. "We can be the first family, Corinne. I will be your new mother. And every creature on this island will be under our spell! If you come willingly, you will lose nothing. You will have your own thoughts, your own will. You can do as you wish. And you will be powerful. We will both be powerful together. As a family, no one will be able to stop us. Imagine being able to do anything you want!"

Severine's eyes glistened with greed at the thought, and Corinne trembled. "But if you refuse to join me," Severine said as her muscles and her hand tightened even more, "you will be a mindless drone, just like the rest of them. Just like your father will be soon. It will be a shame for me to lose all of your wonderful talent—" Severine stopped herself.

In that moment, Severine's eyes widened with shock, as if she had let something slip, but she took a breath and her face returned to its previous sneer. "I will get rid of you if I have to. I don't care if you are my own sister's child."

Corinne's skin prickled and her heart thrummed. She tried to make her face look as if she was thinking hard. "I could do anything?" she said softly.

Severine's grip loosened. "Yes. You could. You are like your mother. Like me. You have far more abilities than you can even imagine."

Corinne moved away from the jumbie's hand. "Like what?"

The bark of Severine's face twisted into a grimace that Corinne thought was meant to be a smile. "I can show you."

Severine came closer. As she did, her body shrank down a little. Corinne could see there were insects crawling up and around Severine's body. Hundreds of millipedes and centipedes, cockroaches, and beetles crawled in and out of the crags of her body. They dashed in and out of the fine fur and bored their way through her chest, so that Corinne could see straight through it like an old rotten tree. Corinne's stomach turned, but she tried not to show it. Instead, she backed up toward one of the windows.

"Sometimes the others would make fun of me because I was faster than they were," Corinne said.

"They were jealous."

"I always felt alone when my father was out on the sea."

"You will never have to feel alone again."

Corinne was right up against the window now. She waited. Severine was almost back down to her usual size. Her green dress skimmed just above her ankles. The holes in her skin began to close. A few insects crawled beneath the surface of her skin. *Just a little bit more,* Corinne thought.

"Will it be like having a mother again?" Corinne asked. She looked steadily at Severine. The jumbie's face had rearranged into something that looked close to joy. A muddy tear trickled down her face and became a large millipede that crawled into a crack in her neck and out again through a hole under her arm. Corinne felt her face twist in disgust. Severine stopped in her tracks and narrowed her eyes at Corinne. Then she looked at where Corinne was standing.

"Get away from the window," she said.

Corinne pretended not to understand. "What do you mean?" She pressed her fingers against the shutter and got ready to fling it open.

"Get away from that window!" Severine screamed and lunged for Corinne.

Corinne jumped out of the way and swung the window open in one movement. The light hit Severine full in the face and she clattered to the floor like a pile of firewood as she tried to avoid it.

Severine pulled back up to her full height, towering over Corinne. Insects crawled in a frenzy up and around her body. "Fine! You will be just like him soon," Severine said, pointing to Pierre. "It would have been nice to show you how to use your gifts. Nicole would have liked that. She should have taught them to you, but perhaps she thought you were too weak. It's a pity, Corinne. We could have been a family."

Corinne did not like the way Severine said her mother's name, like it was a revolting taste on her tongue. "I am not your family. My mama was nothing like you. Everyone loved her. She was lovely and kind. She was—"

"She was a jumbie, Corinne, same as me. And she lied to everyone. Everyone who loved her had no idea who she really was. So you choose your side wisely."

Still shaking, Corinne took a deep breath and tried to sound strong. "I will fight you," she said. But her voice cracked.

"You are very much like them," Severine said. "Ungrateful. My sister saved their kind. She took off their chains and brought them to the island and how did they repay her? By forgetting. In mere days, they started to cut down our trees to build their own homes. Then they set fire to our forests to make space to grow their food. A few years later, they told their children that we were monsters and tried to get rid of us. But now it's our time to turn things back. The people will become jumbies like us, or they will die. And your mother isn't here to convince me otherwise."

"We will *not* let you," Corinne said in a more determined voice.

Severine shrugged. "Then your fate will be worse than his." She pointed to Pierre. "I was right. You are more trouble than you're worth."

Corinne grabbed her papa around the waist and tried to hoist him out of the chair. He was much too large and heavy and they both fell on the floor. She got up and began to pull him away, but Severine grabbed his other hand and pulled Pierre back into his chair. Then she picked Corinne up by the neck. Corinne struggled and kicked at the air as Severine's fingers began to squeeze tighter and tighter around her throat.

Suddenly, Severine's eyes grew wide. She dropped Corinne and looked at her palm. A small oval was burned into it, the same shape and size of the stone on Corinne's necklace. Severine stepped back with a look of fear on her face.

Corinne rose to her feet, ripped off her necklace, and held it in front of Severine, trying to drive her out of the house. But it was not enough. Severine caught her by the wrist and twisted her hand around until Corinne was forced to drop the necklace onto the floor. Then Severine dragged Corinne to the front door and flung her outside. She landed with a thud at the bottom of the orange tree her mama had planted. Corinne wiped away some tears, which fell on the soil above Mrs. Rootsingh's sari silk.

Just then, the brothers and Dru arrived, gasping to catch their breaths from running. They hurried to help Corinne.

Severine stood in the shade of the porch and held out the necklace by its string, unbothered by Dru and the boys. "You see, Corinne? I have your father, and now I have your mother too. The time of people is over. It's *my* time again." Her wicked laugh echoed off the trees. "I will show you whose house this is." Then Severine muttered something in a strange language. Immediately, the ground began to shake beneath them. Long ropes of green broke out of the earth, growing in every direction and sprouting bright orange thorns that glistened with a thick, foul-smelling liquid.

Bouki put his hands over his nose and mouth. "It smells like something rotten!"

Corinne grabbed the back of his shirt and Dru's hand as she scrambled out of the way. Malik had already started running for the road. The four of them barely had time to scramble out of the way as the thorn bush grew up and out and the yard was completely blocked off from the road. There they stood and watched the thick vine wind its way around the entire house, even covering it overhead.

Dru moved forward to get a better look.

"No!" Corinne shouted, just as a vine swung out. Malik pulled Dru out of the way of the vine as it whipped the air where her face had just been.

A bird flew over the house. Another vine lashed out and smacked the bird, which dropped to the ground in front of them. The four quickly backed away from the dead animal.

"What did I tell her, brother?" Bouki said. "Didn't I say she needed a plan?"

Malik nodded.

Corinne stared as thoughts raced through her head: About her father sitting like an empty shell inside the house. Severine being her mama's sister. The way Severine had been burned by the stone necklace.

The brothers looked on as she clutched at the space on her chest where the necklace had been. Malik tugged at her clothes and tried to pull her away from the house.

"What did she do to your father?" Dru asked.

"He doesn't know me," Corinne said. Tears rolled out of her eyes and got soaked up by the dirt at her feet. "He looks like Papa, but he isn't."

"We have to get out of here," Bouki said. He took Corinne's hand and pulled her along behind him.

< 126 >

"She says it's her island," Corinne whispered. "She says she's going to take it back."

"What does she mean by *that*?" Dru asked. "Corinne?"

Corinne stopped and looked at her friends gravely. "It means we have to fight."

Severine wanted to take the island but corinne stands up to her, so severine throws her outside then the house is consumed by vines.

< 127 >

23

The Call

Pierre remained trapped inside himself, unmoving and unthinking. Severine rushed around preparing another pot of stew for him. Until the magic took full hold, she had to keep feeding it to him. She couldn't risk losing him, not now. Not after her sister's child had refused her. She grumbled as she worked, irritated that she had let the girl go.

"I should have found a way to change the child first," Severine muttered.

With the child's magic on her side, turning the rest of the people on the island would have been simpler. But now—now they would fight. Severine didn't mind

< 128 >

the fighting, but she did mind losing her own kind. She shoved a spoonful of stew into Pierre's mouth.

"Well, they will lose too," she said aloud. "At least I have you." Severine dabbed a dribble of stew from Pierre's lips. She looked at him tenderly.

In spite of everything that had gone wrong, she would still get a family. Corinne would eventually follow her father. Severine had noticed they could not be without each other for long. In two more nights, the magic would have permanent hold on Pierre and he and Severine would be sealed together. He would bring his daughter to their side. Eventually, Severine would release Pierre from the magic. He might come to love her as he had loved her sister. But before any of that happened, she had to take care of the people of the island.

Only two nights to wait, but in the silent house, restlessness settled on Severine. She wanted the people turned faster. "Why wait two more nights to begin?" she wondered. "I have an army willing to do as I say. And if Corinne sees what we jumbies can do if she doesn't cooperate, maybe she will join us on her own." She went to the window and sang in a voice only understood by jumbies:

Drowned in water, scorched in sun,
Tonight your time is finally done.
Silent children come and fight,
The people's end begins tonight!

She fed Pierre another spoonful and patted his lips dry. "There now," she said. "That wasn't so bad, was it? And now, I should take care of your wife."

She picked up Nicole's necklace by the string, careful not to touch the stone. It felt heavy under her fingers, not because of the stone itself, but because she understood its magic. She felt its power as soon as it touched her skin. It was Forming Magic, an ancient power that was created at the same time that the very earth was made. It was bigger and more powerful than she herself—more powerful than anything she had ever known. She wondered how her sister had come by it, how she had handled it, and if it was the thing that had allowed her to live among people for as long as she had. Severine was tempted to try to use the magic herself, but she knew that this magic was dangerous even for her. How then could her sister have given it to a child, who wore it so casually around her neck? She cringed at the thought that those boys had tied it around an agouti's tail and set it free in the forest.

"The poor little creature," Severine said to herself as she went out of the house and into the shadowy trees. "It was probably so afraid when it felt this magic tied to its body."

As she walked through the forest, the creatures she passed felt the power of the magic in her hands. A family of lappe trembled among the shadows. The large rodents' white spots blended with the few spots of sunlight that came through the mahogany forest, and their whiskers trembled like the grass at Severine's feet. Even the hummingbirds ceased to dart around the orchids that twined around tree trunks. Everything lay still. In the thickest part of the mahogany forest, where no human could ever walk, Severine returned to her jumbie self. In the open air, her body looked less like the beautiful woman who appeared at the market and more like a tangle of wood and vines, crawling with insects. But her form flickered and faded like a candle as she passed through solid rock and closely knotted trees.

She muttered to herself as she went. "If *I* had it all this time, I would have found the right way to use it. The island could already be mine."

Severine knew that her sister would have known she would use the magic this way. It was no wonder she had given the necklace to Corinne.

"How long had you been lying, sister?" Severine asked. "You fooled us all."

Severine reached the highest point on the island. The cliff overlooked the same bay where Pierre fished. She chose a rock that jutted out over the water and secured the necklace there, far from the child. Now it would be safe until Severine understood how to unlock its full magic. It was a delicate thing. And once used, it could never be used again.

As Severine walked back down through the trees, she

whispered another message to the jumbies in their language, telling them:

> *Children, children, stand on guard.*
> *No one enters through our yard.*
> *Sharpen claws and sticks and stones.*
> *Tonight we shall retake our home.*

Jumbies emerged from the trees to listen to her plan. The forest came alive with sounds of slithering, cracking, scratching, and shuffling as each of them got ready. Already, the sun was slipping toward the sea. Soon, the battle would begin.

I think the battle will be crazy and the jubies will use all of there power... And the humans will get the witch and she will help them.

24

The Lagahoo

From its perch on the rock, Nicole's necklace dangled in the sea breeze and shimmered in the sun. Its gleam shone over the shore, where it made the fishermen squint as they drew in their nets for the day. Farther up the coast, where Corinne and her friends sat, the light traced a path in the sand up to their feet. Malik spotted the necklace first. He pointed. Corinne saw it next and immediately knew what it was. It seemed to pull at her, to call her to it.

Corinne had not wanted to get too far from her house, and none of the others were willing to leave her. She sat in the sand all day feeling helpless, but now her hands flew up to her chest, where her mama's necklace had been for as long as she could remember. She remembered the day that her mama had untied the string from her own neck and put it around hers. The string was so long, the stone fell to her stomach. She remembered that her mama had told her to guard it, that it would protect her, but in her memory it wasn't her mama's voice that she heard saying it. It was her father's voice telling her the story. Corinne hated that she couldn't remember how her mama had said her very last words.

"I have to get the necklace back," Corinne said to Dru and the boys.

Malik shook his head.

Bouki looked up. "How? No one can get up there."

The knot inside Corinne pulled tight. She leaned over with her hands on her knees. "It's the only way," she said to them. "You don't have to help me. This is my problem."

"We are all in this together now, aren't we brother?" Bouki said.

Malik patted Corinne's shoulder. She tried to summon up a smile to show them all that she was fine, that she was strong, but she didn't feel that way. She felt angry and alone, even though her friends were there with her. But they weren't her family. She didn't want to stay where she could see the necklace. She started on the road toward town. Dru and the boys followed.

Behind them, the sun slid beneath the ocean and threw the whole island in darkness.

"You should get home, Dru. Your mother will be worried," Corinne said. "I'll go back to the cave with . . ."

A huge creature with a face like a dog and a body nearly as tall as the trees stood in the road panting heavily. A line of saliva dripped from its sharp white teeth. The chains around its neck clinked softly every time it took a breath.

Corinne stood frozen with fear. "Lagahoo!"

All four of them stood rooted to the dirt road as the lagahoo panted at them. Big slops of saliva plopped on the ground from its deep-red mouth. Its teeth were the size of kitchen knives, and they gleamed in the light of the rising moon. All at once, the creature crouched down, about to pounce. Bouki was the fastest to act. He bent down and sprinted away from the creature and toward the red hills. Malik followed his brother. Dru screamed again but ran away from the forest, down the road that led to her village. Only Corinne remained, staring the lagahoo down, not out of bravery but because she didn't know where to run.

The lagahoo growled and jumped into the air. Corinne ducked and ran toward it. The lagahoo soared over her head and landed where Corinne had been, cracking the ground beneath it. The creature snarled with anger and whipped around. Corinne ran.

The lagahoo lurched forward and came toward Corinne at full gallop, dragging its chains behind.

Corinne's muscles screamed from the effort of running,

and she wasn't sure how much longer she could go on. In seconds, she could feel the lagahoo's hot breath against her neck. And then she heard the clank of chains and a strange whimper. Then nothing.

Corinne stopped and turned. The creature stood still. It breathed its hot, foul breath into her face, but something in its eyes spelled distress. It moved back and tried to surge forward again, but its chains had become tangled in the branches of a tamarind tree. The lagahoo tried to struggle forward, and the long brown tamarind fruits knocked together, sounding like an audience applauding its capture.

Warm relief surged from Corinne's head down to her toes. But if this jumbie was out, then so were others. Severine's battle had started. Corinne needed to help her friends. She backed away from the angry lagahoo and ran off toward the village.

Is the lagahoo a jumbi?
I think everyone split up b/c the next chapter is called bauki & Mallik!

25

Bouki and Malik

The brothers ran until their legs burned with effort.
When they were far enough away, they stopped beneath a pink poui tree and tried to catch their breath. Their
rest did not last long.

The sounds of shouting and crying had erupted all
over the island. From every corner, the boys heard the
clank of metal and thuds of hand-to-hand blows. The
fighting seemed dangerously close to their little clearing.

"We have to make it to the cave, brother," Bouki said.

Malik grabbed his hand and pulled him in the other
direction, toward the fighting.

"No, no. We have to go the other way. You don't want us to get killed, do you?"

"Who will kill you?" a woman's voice asked.

Bouki felt a chill all the way to his bones. He looked around, expecting to see Severine, but instead, there was another woman standing there. She had milky brown skin and sea-green eyes, and was, amazingly, nearly as beautiful as Severine herself. She wore a long white gown, elbow-length white gloves, and a broad-brimmed white hat, all of which seemed to glow in the moonlight.

Bouki felt drawn to her. He took a couple of shaky steps in her direction. "Where did you come from?"

The woman pointed out of the clearing to the tops of the mahogany forest. "From there."

"So you're a jumbie?" Bouki asked with a trembling voice. He took another step toward her.

"We're not all so bad," the jumbie said. She reached her arms out to Bouki to draw him closer. "How old are you, little one?" she asked.

"Twelve. But I'm a big twelve," Bouki added when he saw one side of the jumbie's mouth curl up into a mocking smile.

"So I guess you are old enough, then," she said. With her arms out, she kept drawing him nearer.

"For what?" Bouki asked. He turned his head to look for his brother, but Malik was nowhere to be seen.

"Oh, don't worry about him," the jumbie coaxed. "He

ran off. He was too scared of me. But I know you are not. You are a big boy of twelve, and nothing frightens you, eh?"

The wind picked up then and shook the last remnants of the smell of the poui flowers down from the branches. But it stirred up something else: something that smelled sharp and rotting. Bouki's nose wrinkled.

"What is that?" he asked aloud.

"What, dear?" the jumbie asked gently, though her sea-green eyes had become hard, like glass.

"You don't smell that?" Bouki asked. As he did, the wind picked up the ends of the jumbie's long gown and blew them back. There was one sleek brown leg and one hairy cow's foot.

The jumbie tried to rearrange her clothes quickly, but it was too late. Bouki already began to back away. The jumbie's face contorted into an angry grimace, and she grabbed up her skirt and moved toward him. She only made it a few awkward steps when she fell to the ground, stunned.

Bouki gasped as he watched the jumbie writhe in the dirt. Her legs were tied together with rope. Then Malik jumped out of the poui tree holding the other end of the rope. Before the jumbie could untie herself, Malik bound the jumbie's arms to her sides.

"You will leave me here like this?" the jumbie screamed.

Malik nodded.

"I will get you. I promise you I will," the jumbie shouted.

Malik pointed at the rope and shook his head. Then he grabbed his brother's hand and pulled him out of the clearing. They left the jumbie screaming insults. Malik led Bouki toward the sound of the fighting.

"Where are you going, brother?" Bouki asked. "You don't want to run into more like that La Diabless, do you?"

Malik nodded solemnly.

"One of them will certainly kill us," Bouki said.

Malik turned away from his brother and pressed on.

"All right, but if I get killed, I'll haunt you for the rest of your life."

Malik looked back and raised both of his eyebrows.

"Well, I guess if we both get killed, you'll have to hear me complain about it for eternity."

Malik moved out of the clearing and back toward the village with Bouki following behind. In a few minutes, the sound of fighting was sharp in their ears, and the smell of mingled sweat, dirt, and blood hung in the air over the usual nighttime scent of the island. Clouds moved over the moon and threw everything into darkness. The boys bumped into something soft and stumbled to the ground. The clouds parted again and they found themselves on the ground next to a little old woman.

"Sorry, Grandmother," Bouki said quickly. He and Malik reached out to help the old woman back to her feet, but her skin was fire-hot. They both pulled away and shook the heat from their hands. "Are you sick?" Bouki asked. "You should not be out on a night like this, especially if you're not well. Who do you belong to? Maybe we can take you back to your family?" This time he bore the heat of her hand to pull her to her feet. Malik did not touch her.

The old woman smiled, but did not let go of Bouki's hand.

Bouki tried to pull the old lady off, but her grip was like a vice. Bouki began to scream from the pain of the heat.

The old woman began to shudder a little as if she was cold, but the skin around her bones loosened and slid off, revealing a fiery body inside. She was a *soucouyant*—a malicious fireball that would suck the lifeblood out of anyone, even a baby. Her skin pooled around her, leaving Bouki holding the empty shell of her hand. He shuddered and let it fall with a slap against the rest of the discarded skin while the flame-body gathered up into a ball and hovered a few feet above the ground.

The boys turned and ran to the village with the soucouyant just behind them. In the streets all around them, people were fighting jumbies. Bouki and Malik darted around a group of fishermen who had surrounded a lagahoo, battling to take it down with hooks and nets. Bloody claw marks covered one fisherman's arm. Down the road, a small band of douens were crawling all over a house, getting in the windows and doors, with people inside and outside trying to beat them away with brooms, garden rakes, and an oar.

Malik clenched his fists and seemed about to dive into the fight, but Bouki grabbed his arm and dragged him toward Hugo's bakery. The soucouyant was still on their trail. Bouki pushed his brother down next to the outdoor clay oven and crouched beside him. The oven was warm, its coals still burning deep inside. Several feet in front of the boys, the soucouyant hovered in the air. It darted and turned, looking for the boys, casting an orange glow on all of the fighters.

"Fire in front and fire behind, eh brother? Too bad you really can't fight fire with fire," Bouki said.

Suddenly, Malik smiled and patted Bouki hard on the back. Bouki yelped and Malik put his fingers to his lips. The soucouyant made a swift turn and moved in their direction.

Next to the clay oven, there was a metal bucket. Malik picked up Hugo's tongs and reached deep inside the oven for some of the hot coals. He put these into the bucket and took one of Hugo's cloths to hold the bucket carefully. Then he pulled his slingshot out of his pocket.

Bouki saw the slingshot and understood immediately. He got out his own. As they crawled back toward the fighting, they picked up several stones and shoved them into their pockets. When they were finally at the side of the road, they loaded up their slingshots and started to shoot.

The soucouyant backed up at first, but then it barreled toward them in a blur of flame. Just as it was about to engulf the boys, an oar smacked it to the ground. A hefty fisherman stood over the soucouyant as if in a daze. The light from the soucouyant's flame shone in his face, and the boys recognized him as Victor, the same man who had tried to get Corinne out of her father's boat. The soucouyant began to rise from the ground, and Victor lifted his oar to hit it again. A small lagahoo crept up behind Victor and hit him hard on the back. The wood from Victor's oar only caught the outer edges of the flame and passed through.

Bouki pointed at the soucouyant. "Aim for the center of the fireball. Only the outside is flame."

Malik tucked his hair behind his ears and nodded.

The man turned his attention to the lagahoo. He swung and his oar broke against the lagahoo's arm, leaving a sharp pointed end. He jabbed the point at the lagahoo while Bouki pummeled the soucouyant with rocks from his slingshot. Malik scrambled closer to the fisherman and the lagahoo. With the cloth wrapped around his hand, he loaded a hot coal into his slingshot, aimed, and fired at the lagahoo's body.

The lagahoo spun around, roaring from pain. Its fur began to smoke.

Bouki raised his brow and smirked. "Two in one!" he yelled at Victor. He gestured for him to use his oar like a bat on the soucouyant. "Send it there!" he yelled and pointed toward the smoking lagahoo.

Victor smiled and nodded and got the broken oar ready to swing like a cricket bat.

The soucouyant lunged toward them both. Victor swung and connected. The ball of fire sailed, hissing through the air. It struck the lagahoo's fur. The monster roared and screamed in an explosion of flames. Victor and Bouki cheered as both the lagahoo and the soucouyant fell in a fiery heap. When the fire died out, a smoldering pile of ash was all that was left of the two jumbies.

The brothers leaned against each other, panting.

"That is not the last of them," Victor said sternly. "Go home and leave the fighting to the grown-ups."

The boys stood up straight and armed their slingshots again. Bouki set his jaw and gave Victor a look that showed he and his brother weren't going anywhere.

"All right then, men. Let's go," Victor yelled and charged with his plank down the road, where they quickly found another fight with yet another lagahoo. With a fierce yell, Victor raced in to help the men and women with rakes and garden hoes who were fighting the beast.

The boys turned to find someone else to help, and spotted a small band of douens that had holed up behind the market wall. The creatures hurled huge boulders at

< 144 >

some frightened villagers, who huddled, trapped, against another wall. The boys loaded stone after stone into their slingshots and fired, but with no effect on the douens. The villagers ducked, but the douens' rocks came fast. Many of the villagers were bleeding from where they had been hit.

In the midst of the flying rocks, Malik ran out and stood between the douens and the villagers.

"Come back here!" Bouki shouted.

Malik moved closer to the douens.

"No!" Bouki shouted.

The douens ran out, tumbling over themselves to try to grab Malik first. As they got closer to Malik, they shouted, "Oh, oh, oh" louder and faster.

Bouki was about to lunge forward to put himself in front of his brother. But then Malik sprang into action. He ran toward the villagers. The douens were left exposed. Now the trapped villagers swarmed forward and surrounded the douens.

Bouki clutched his brother's arm and tugged him away while the villagers fought the douens hand to hand. The boys stayed on the road this time, since all of their usual paths seemed to be blocked.

"Are we being followed, brother?" Bouki asked.

Malik nodded and pointed behind. A figure was moving toward them near the side of the road. It wore a gray shirt long enough to hide its feet. Bouki narrowed his eyes and loaded his slingshot. Malik did the same, though he didn't aim just yet. As the figure got closer, Bouki dropped to one knee and pulled the slingshot taut, aiming for the head. Just as he was about to let go, Malik jostled him and the rock flew wide, missing the mark completely.

"Why'd you do that?" Bouki pushed him.

Malik pointed and ran to the person in the gray shirt. Bouki scrambled to his feet and followed. "Corinne! You're alive! How? That lagahoo . . ."

"It was luck. Its chains got caught in a tree. There are jumbies everywhere."

"We know. The good news is, you can destroy them," Bouki said. But when Corinne began to smile, he added, "But it's not easy. It's not easy at all."

Corinne gave him a firm nod. "Where's Dru?"

Bouki and Malik frowned. "She's not with you?" Bouki asked.

Corinne swallowed hard as the darkness seemed to thicken around them.

I think she got
alterd.

< 146 >

26

Quiet Morning

There was no way for Corinne and the boys to find Dru. They were hemmed in by jumbies and villagers fighting. Instead, the three found their way back to the baker's outdoor oven and slumped to the ground in a heap, leaning against each other to keep their backs and heads upright in case of attack. But in moments, they had all fallen asleep from exhaustion.

Several hours later, all three of them woke up on flour sacks on the floor of the bakery. Hugo, the baker, was asleep on a chair barring the front door. The thick, oar-like pallet that he used to put the bread into the brick oven was lying across his lap. The flat end was cracked and splintered. Hugo didn't look much better. His arm was slashed in places as if he had been mauled by a lagahoo.

While the baker continued to sleep, Corinne opened one of the windows, and she and the boys slipped outside. In the bright midday light, the remains of the battle were revealed in sharp, horrible detail. The village was in shambles. Torn bits of cloth lay everywhere. Dust circled in the air. Stones, broken pieces of wood, tufts of fur, branches, bricks, burned-out torches, and broken lanterns were strewn along the road, in yards, and around the open market. In some places, little piles of ash with tiny wisps of smoke still curling above them began to blow away in the breeze. Every now and then, the children stepped over gory tracks where the wounded had been dragged off into the woods. Whether the victims were human or jumbie, they could not tell. Although the sun was already high in the sky, the three of them were the only ones outside. The island had never been so quiet.

"They're gone for now," Corinne said. "We have until tonight to think of what to do."

"What can we do?" Bouki said. "They are stronger than us. They can make giant killer weeds grow up out of the ground in seconds. They have claws and razor-sharp teeth and fur."

"Everything has a weakness," Corinne said. "Remember, Dru said they can't come out during the day."

"Severine can," Dru said.

"Dru!" Corinne rushed to hug her. "You're okay!"

Dru didn't hug her back. Her hair was unbraided and waved in the wind, and there was a strange look in her eyes.

"What happened?" Corinne asked.

"They were everywhere," Dru said. "I made it all the way home, and I peeped out of a hole in the wall near my bed. I saw them come out of the forest and start banging down doors and fighting with my neighbors. Then a little band of douens started to pitch marbles in the street. My neighbor Allan . . ." she paused and looked at Corinne. "He came out to play with them. I wanted to scream at him not to go, but I didn't want them to know where I was. So I just watched. As soon as he picked up a marble to pitch, they started saying 'Oh, oh, oh' and next thing, Allan was saying it too."

Corinne gasped. "What happened?"

"His mother came out and tried to call him back. So then the jumbies knew his name. They called him, and he followed them into the forest. His mother called him again, but he couldn't go to her."

"Why not?" Bouki asked.

"When he turned back toward his mother, his legs didn't turn with him. They were still walking toward the forest while the rest of him was facing his mother. I stopped looking then. I could still hear all the fighting, but I couldn't watch anymore."

Corinne tried to shake off the cold feeling that was crawling up her spine. Then she whispered, "I'm sorry."

Dru cast an accusing eye at Corinne, but said nothing.

Malik hung his left arm at his side and hobbled for a few steps.

"That's no use. We tried to talk to the witch before," Corinne said. "She didn't want to help."

Malik waved his hand at the destruction all around them.

"You're right, brother," Bouki said. "Things are different now."

"The white witch doesn't care," Corinne said.

"Maybe it's you she doesn't want to help," Dru said. "You were the one who went running into the mahogany forest, where everyone knows there are jumbies. You were the one who had that jumbie in your house. Maybe the witch just didn't want to help you." She bit down hard on her trembling lip.

"It's not my fault that Miss Severine followed me out of the forest. And if you're looking for somebody to blame for sending me in there . . ." She pointed a finger at Bouki.

"Me? How was I supposed to know that stupid 'gouti would go that way?"

Malik stamped his foot so hard that the curls on his head shook. He pointed toward the forest and then back at the village. Then he put his hands on his hips.

"Okay, you're right, Malik," Corinne said. "They could come back again. So how do we find the witch?"

I think the witch will go cast spells.

27

The Swamp

No human had ever seen the witch's house. But everyone knew that it was hidden in a swamp of stinking water, surrounded by mangrove trees so thick that some said they were enchanted to make sure no one got through. No one had ever attempted the trek to see the witch in her lair—until now.

Corinne, Dru, Bouki, and Malik journeyed north around the coast of the island toward the mouth of the largest river. About midafternoon, they finally heard the sound of churning water where the river mingled with the sea. They turned and followed it deeper into the island. The farther they went, the more they got crowded in by mangrove trees. The children waded in the water, swatting away thick swarms of flies, because the big, gray roots were too dense on either bank for even their small feet. The water was not much better. Mangrove roots arched down like giant, aged fingers and tripped them as they walked. Then, as the trees began to come in even closer, growing directly out of the river, the water became still and turned to swamp.

The murky, greenish water of the swamp seemed to stretch on forever around them.

Corinne stopped and looked around at the still water and the ancient trees with their tangled roots. She held her nose and breathed through her mouth to avoid the stink. Besides the horrible stench, there was no way to tell how deep the water would get, or behind what grove of trees the witch's hut stood, or even what creatures watched, hidden in the trees or under the water. It took her several heartbeats before she could take another step forward. The others waited for her. They moved only when she did.

Bits of thick, brown, oily muck clung to their clothes as they went. Behind them, they left a trail of muck-free, greenish water.

"Something's on me, it's on me!" Dru screamed. "Get it off!"

"Stop it. You're splashing the slime on me, Dru!" Bouki said.

"Get it off!" Dru screamed.

"There's nothing on you," Corinne said to Dru. "You're imagining things."

"You got nasty swamp water in my mouth!" Bouki complained. "Stop with all that splashing!"

Corinne put both her hands on Dru's shoulders as much to steady her own quaking body as to calm Dru down. "We'll be out soon. It's not so bad. Look. It's clearing up ahead."

Malik tapped his brother's shoulder and pointed out a snake curled on a branch overhead. Corinne saw it too. It was barely noticeable, only a slightly paler shade of green than the leaves around it. Then it unfurled and stretched itself toward the water.

"Looks like we're going to be in that clearing sooner than you think," Bouki said. He cut through the swamp as fast as he could go, splashing up vile-smelling water.

Malik followed close behind. Corinne trailed a little, pulling Dru along. The long, green snake touched down in the water. It began to slither toward them in a curving line over the surface of the swamp. It was fast.

All four of them screamed and beat a rapid path away from the snake.

"Come on! Come on!" Bouki shouted from up ahead.

When they were finally away from the trees, the ground beneath them dropped suddenly and they were forced to swim. Bouki struck out for the middle of the swamp with Malik close behind. Corinne pushed Dru ahead of her and followed, paddling hard. They cleared the mangrove and the muck, but they all continued to swim frantically until Bouki called, "It's okay. It's gone."

They were all covered in nasty-smelling slime, and wet, cold, and panting from exhaustion. The witch's house was still nowhere in sight. "We're wasting time," Corinne said. "We should go back."

Malik reached his hand out and pointed behind her. There, in the middle of the clearing, was a tiny island. It was not much more than a muddy mound rising out of the center of the swamp with a small shack on top.

Corinne smiled. "Good eye, Malik!"

Corinne led the way toward the little island. Near its shore a mossy row of rocks rose out of the water and made a path toward the witch's hut.

It was hard for them to pull themselves up onto the slippery rocks. Several times they lost their footing and wound up back in the water. Only Malik seemed to make progress, as if he had grips on the soles of his feet.

"How does the old witch do it?" Bouki asked after he fell in yet again.

"She's a witch. She uses magic," Dru said.

"Maybe the rocks are only slippery for us. Maybe when she is walking on them, it's a regular road," Bouki said a moment before he fell back into the water up to his neck.

As Corinne slipped into the water again, Malik moved

past her on nimble feet. "How are you doing that?" she asked. But Malik only snickered.

Bouki got back up on the rocks. "She does this with a tray of potions balanced on her head?"

"Like I said, it's magic," Dru said.

"I could use some magic," Bouki complained.

At last they all made it to the witch's door. Corinne knocked three times, hard. They dripped swamp water on the witch's front step and waited.

The crooked door wobbled open and the witch peered through it. She studied the slime-covered children carefully. "You again?" she asked. Her voice grated like a boat scraping along gravel. She turned back inside the shack and left the door open.

Corinne watched the bright colors of her housedress darken in the shadows of the hut. She hesitated at the door.

"I won't eat you," the witch said from inside. She began to laugh, but ended up coughing instead.

Corinne went in first, and the others followed her. The house was only one room. On shelves along the crooked walls, there were glass, clay, and wooden containers of various shapes and sizes. The floor was bare wood rubbed smooth from countless years of the old woman's shuffling feet.

The witch gestured to a rough-hewn table and bench in the middle of the room. "Sit." She moved to the opposite side and returned to filling and sorting the ingredients in her potions.

"Why wouldn't you help us when we came to you in the market yesterday?" Corinne demanded.

"I didn't know then what she wanted," the witch replied. Her shoulders drooped toward the floor. Her deep-brown skin, which already had lines and grooves like the bark of a tree, seemed to crease even more deeply.

"I tried to warn you," Corinne said. "I knew she was going to do something to hurt us all."

Dru put her hands on her hips. "*You* knew?"

"Well, my friends knew," Corinne corrected herself. "But I came to you and you did nothing."

The witch shuffled over to a shelf. As she went, her long yellow toenails clicked on the wooden floor. She scratched at the shiny brown bald spots between her white braids. At her side, her left arm hung withered and limp. She didn't seem like someone powerful, someone who could help.

With some difficulty, the witch rolled a piece of paper into a funnel with her good arm and poured red seeds into small bottles. She stuck a cork in each one and put them on a tray. Malik reached out a finger toward a slip of paper that held a tiny hill of black pods.

"Do you like your fingers the way they are?" the witch snapped.

Malik froze. The witch shook her head at him and he pulled his hand back into his lap. In that moment, she looked like her previous self: powerful, self-assured, and able.

"So what do you want me to do now?" she asked without looking at any of them.

"I need to get past the jumbies," Corinne said.

"Ha!" the witch replied with contempt. "How do you plan on doing that?"

"Can't you help me? You get past them all the time."

"The jumbies don't have anything to fear from me, and there's nothing I have that they want," the witch said. "I also don't go around fighting them and trying to set fire to their homes, so they trust me. If you can say the same thing, then you can also get past them."

"Isn't there some trick?" Corinne asked.

The witch shook her head and her white braids tossed around.

"Then can't you just get rid of the jumbies?" Corinne asked.

"Me? You people have too much faith in what I can do."

"You could if you wanted to," Corinne said. "What are all these for?" She gestured to the bottles, seeds, and leaves on the table.

"Some people need these things."

"Right now, people need to get rid of all those jumbies. What do you have here for that?"

"Nothing," said the white witch.

"Severine has put some kind of magic on my papa. He

< 157 >

doesn't even know what's happening around him. And now there's a poisonous vine wrapped around my house. What do you have for that?"

"You have any jumbie weed killer on this table?" Bouki asked with a grin. He nudged his brother and Dru. But no one laughed. The witch shot him a nasty look and he pretended to smooth out a knot on the wood table.

"I told you that was a bad one. And now she has completely taken over your house?" The witch shook her head and clucked her tongue. "Women and men live together all the time," she said finally. "You should try to get along with your new mother."

"She's not my mother!" Corinne shouted. She clenched her fists to stop them from shaking. "Do you understand? She's taking my papa. She's changing him. You're the only person who can help. Don't tell me you're just going to stand there and do nothing! I can't stand around and watch him become a . . ." Corinne hesitated.

"A jumbie," Dru finished, with a firm nod.

Corinne shot her an angry look. "He isn't a jumbie. He doesn't know who he is. I could probably make him better if I could only get into my house when she isn't there."

"Past her poison weed?" the witch asked.

Corinne folded her arms around herself. "You must have something here I can use. She's stronger than me. And she's turned on everyone else. Didn't you hear them all last night? This is our island and their kind are trying to take over."

"Their kind?" the witch asked. "What kind is that?" She looked at Corinne beneath one cocked, white eyebrow.

"The kind of things that came out of the forest last night," Corinne said slowly.

"Their kind, your kind, is there a difference?"

"They are trying to kill us!" Dru said.

"*They* belong to this island, child. You cannot get rid of them. They are part of it. You don't like it when someone moves into your house for an afternoon," the witch said to Corinne. "How would you like it if someone moved in, shoved you and your family into the deepest pockets of the island, and refused to leave for a couple hundred years? And what if those new people forgot that you were even there, and when they found you again, they feared you and tried to kill you off? How would you like that?"

Corinne looked down at her hands in her lap. Severine had told her the same thing. With a small voice, she said, "They're not like regular people." But she understood about losing her home, and she was willing to fight for it, the same as Severine.

"I'm not like regular people, either," the witch said. "Will you be trying to get rid of me next?"

Corinne searched the witch's face. "How are you different?"

"I'm as different as you are," she said, eyeing Corinne.

Corinne stiffened. Her eyes darted to her friends to see if they understood what the witch meant.

"They're taking children," Dru pleaded. "They're probably going to get these two boys next. They don't even have parents to look after them."

"Hey!" Bouki said.

"It's true. You don't," Dru said. But she didn't want to scare Malik too much, so she smiled at him and patted his hand a little.

"Look," Corinne said. "We know Severine wanted something from one of your little bottles here. Whatever magic she used on my papa probably came from right here."

"You made this mess." Bouki banged his fist on the wood table. Some of the bottles wobbled and clinked together. "So you help us fix it."

He tried to hold the witch's gaze. But when her eyes burned into his, he looked down at the table again and put his hands in his lap.

"You think I had something to do with that? You're wrong," the witch said. "She didn't need any help turning your father. Men are turned by pretty faces every minute of every day."

Bouki nodded. "I told her that, didn't I, brother?" he asked Malik softly.

Malik didn't even blink in response to his brother.

"Then what did she come to you for?" Corinne asked.

"She came to me for a way to stay on the outside. Her kind can't live too long away from their own element."

Corinne and Dru exchanged a look. "How could you help her but not help us?" Corinne asked. "Now she's taken over my house. My mama's house. She's killing my papa!" The words burned her throat.

The witch sighed deeply. "It is my vow. I cannot take sides. If I help one side, I have to help the other. So it's better to stay out of it entirely. I have helped your side plenty. I've done all I can do."

"What happens to you if you take sides?" Corinne asked.

"You see how my arm has shriveled up," the witch said. "Useless."

Bouki sucked his teeth, *chups*. "That happened to you when you went swimming in the river that day, when you nearly drowned yourself."

"You're not too smart, are you, boy?" the witch sneered. "Do you imagine I could have lived surrounded by water for over a hundred years and never have learned how to swim?" She turned her attention to Malik. "It must be very frustrating living with a dunce like this one."

Malik's face broke into a brief smile that disappeared when he saw his brother's hurt face.

"Can't you fix your arm?" Corinne asked.

"I don't have a remedy for her magic," the witch said. "It's an old magic, far beyond what I know."

"What about my papa?"

The witch shook her head.

"And what would happen to me? What if I tried?" Corinne asked in a low voice.

"Ah, I see. So you already know what you are, then." The witch saw the confused looks on the faces of the other children. "But you have not told your friends yet?"

Corinne looked down at the table. "I don't believe it," she said softly.

"You believe it a little. I can tell. And you should. It's true. Your mother, Nicole, she was a jumbie just like Severine, or the green woman, or whatever it is you call her. And she came to me once asking for help—"

Corinne shook her head. "No."

"Only she didn't tell me exactly what kind of help, so I'm not sure that what I gave her worked the way she wanted it to. And when she didn't go home, the rest of her jumbie kin must have thought that living among people did her in."

"Please. Stop."

"But she lived, for a time anyway. She lived long enough to have you. And now somehow, her sister has found out about you, and she sees her chance again. They were a pair, you see. Severine needs her family back. She is stronger with more of her kind surrounding her."

Corinne remembered what Severine told her about how powerful they would be when they were a family again. She looked at her friends, at the way their mouths had gone slack with shock. She slapped the table with her palms and stood. "Stop!"

"My stopping won't change things. She will get rid of every single creature that stands in her way. And do you know why she's doing it? It's partly for losing the sister she loved—and she is capable of love—and partly because she never wanted people on this island in the first place, but mostly it's because now she knows that she can have an even larger jumbie family. Because someone like you exists. One half-jumbie like me is just a fluke, an accident, but two of us . . ."

On either side of Corinne, the children's eyes widened with horror. Corinne kept shaking her head and hands as if she could toss the words back out, un-hear the sound of Severine's voice telling her that she was part of the jumbie world, that she was the same as all the other creatures in the forest, and the witch telling her that it was all true.

"That can't be," Dru said into the silence.

The witch raised one white eyebrow. "Did it ever strike you as strange that her house is the only one that is built so close to the forest? And when the jumbies do venture out at night, they have never visited it, even though it is the closest?"

Dru slid away from Corinne in tiny movements along the bench.

"You're not going to help us, are you?" Bouki asked as Corinne stood furious and silent facing the witch.

The witch pressed her good fist against her hip. "Everybody thinks they need magic. Everybody wants answers. Get rid of this boil. Help me find money. She doesn't love me anymore. Why won't my cane stalks grow as tall as my neighbor's? Everybody wants a fast, easy solution. Maybe if you took care of your skin, you wouldn't have gotten the boil in the first place. Maybe if you worked harder you would make more money. Maybe that person isn't the right one for you. Maybe if you found a better way to farm, your crop would come up better. But nobody wants to hear those things. They want a bottle. Instant success! Something to drink, or sprinkle, or spill on the ground. They want magic from nothing. Magic doesn't come from nothing. It comes from somewhere. And it isn't so extraordinary. It's just work. It's just using your head and your heart." She grabbed a seed and put it on the table, then grabbed a cleaver and hoisted it into the air. The children shrank back. She brought the cleaver down on the seed, slicing it in two.

"Look. See what's inside? Nothing. It's just a seed. But put it in the ground and water it, and give it what it needs, and something extraordinary happens. A seed is a promise—"

"A guarantee," Corinne added, remembering her mama's words. She closed her eyes, and this time, she could almost hear her mother speak.

"The real magic is in what you do with it," the witch said. She put the two halves of the seed into Corinne's hand. "It grows roots. It becomes hard to break. You feel it growing. You see when it's about to sprout, and bud, and bear fruit. You can feel it inside you. You know it like you know something is watching you from the shadows. It's instinct. This is your magic. Mine is of no use to you." The witch pushed Corinne's fingers closed around the seed and turned back to her work. "What Severine took from me is probably wearing off already. If she hasn't figured out a way to live on the outside, she's going to have to go back home soon. That's the good news. I can't help her anymore. I won't."

"But she isn't just leaving," Corinne said. "She's taking my papa with her."

"That is the bad news," the witch agreed. "She's going to take as many of you with her as she can."

Corinne said, "You told me my mama came to you once. If she never came back it means that she figured out a way to live in the open on her own. How did she do it?"

"She had your father's love, and love is powerful. You can endure most things for love. It's like planting a seed. Every day it gets stronger and stronger. Every day it grew inside her."

"You mean like a baby?" Corinne asked. "You mean I helped my mama to live on the outside?"

"It had to be you. She didn't have any other magic. But

it couldn't have been easy for her. She fell in love and every day she had to push past the pain of living where she didn't belong. But like everything else, the harder something is, the stronger you become. You must have made her strong. Mothers are like that. Their children strengthen them. There was no trick."

"So how do we get rid of Severine?" Bouki asked. "She doesn't have any children growing inside her, does she?" He screwed up his face in disgust.

The witch laughed and then coughed again. "She doesn't need to. La Diabless, the lagahoo, the douens, even the soucouyant, they are all her children already. What you are dealing with is much stronger than all of them. She is an ancient. She is their mother. She created all of them, and they make her strong. You can't get rid of her, especially if she has found a partner to replace her sister."

"My papa?" Corinne said with horror.

Malik nudged Corinne gently, then he pulled one of his slingshot stones from his pocket to show her.

"My mama's stone pendant," Corinne said. "It hurt Severine when she touched it. She took it away from me and put it up on the cliff."

The white witch spilled a little of the dust she was pouring. "What kind of stone?"

"Small, black, round," Corinne answered. "It must be important. All I need is a path through the mahogany forest to get it back. You have to be able to do that much."

The witch faced her with fierce eyes. "You keep forgetting about my arm. I am a half-jumbie. I vowed never to pick sides, and for that, I was able to gather my magic and live a long life. But now that I have broken my word, you see the consequences are harsh. I don't have much longer to live." She laughed, long and bitter. "What do you think happened that day when the four of you were swimming in the river? What do you think withered my arm that afternoon? What do you imagine was trying to reach you from beneath the water?" She watched the truth dawn on each of the children at her table. "Yes. If I had left Severine to drown you all, maybe she would have been satisfied with that. Maybe she would never have learned that this little one here was a child like me. Maybe she wouldn't have figured out that people weren't as strong as she once thought. Then she would have returned to the forest and never come out again. I chose not to sacrifice you. But maybe I chose wrong."

"She knew what I was already," Corinne said. "She knew when she followed me out of the forest and to my mama's grave on All Hallow's Eve." Corinne remembered Hugo's warning that other beings walked the earth that night. She had not believed in those things then. Even Dru had warned her to be careful of Severine. If she had listened all along . . . but it was too late now.

The witch shrugged. "No matter. But now you are going to have to choose as well. You have inherited your

< 167 >

mother's magic. She protected you from the creatures in the forest for as long as she could. I don't know how her protection was broken, or what made Severine follow you out. But now she knows. That means you can join her, you can try to fight her, or you can stand by and watch while the rest of the island figures it out. But whatever you choose will come with a price. You will lose something: your father, your friends, or your freedom."

"I will fight her," Corinne said.

The white witch nodded. "A noble choice. But you will lose."

"What about my papa?"

"She needs a partner. Someone to be her real family, not just another jumbie she can order around. The spell she worked on him would have had to be different than the usual tricks. She would have used a lot of magic. It would work slowly." The witch looked past them as if trying to figure it out. "Three nights. Then her magic will take hold. Don't let the sun rise after the third night."

"It has already been two," Corinne said.

The witch pointed out of the window. The sun was already descending in the sky. The third night was coming. "If you plan to do something, make it quick."

I think corinne will win the battle/fight!

28

Separate Ways

The four left the swamp and made their way along the coast, away from the witch's shack. The river had mercifully washed most of the swamp stench from their clothes and hair, and the sun was beginning to dry them off. None of them spoke. Corinne noticed that Dru hung back a little from the group. She stopped suddenly and turned around to face Dru.

"What are you doing?" Corinne asked.

"Nothing," Dru said softly.

"Why aren't you walking with the rest of us?"

"I'm walking."

"Not with us."

"I'm right behind you," Dru protested. She pulled a long lock of hair to the front and began to play with it.

Bouki and Malik turned to look at the girls. Malik nudged his brother, and Bouki rolled his eyes to the sky.

Corinne asked, "Are you trying to keep an eye on me? Do you think I'm going to work some kind of magic on you?"

"No," Dru said, though she didn't sound too sure.

"You think I'm just like Severine or the douens who took your friend away. You're afraid of me now, aren't you?"

"I'm not scared," Dru said.

"You're scared of everything," Corinne said.

"I'm not," Dru insisted, but her lip began to quiver, so she bit down on it. "I came with you to see the witch, didn't I?"

"You stayed the closest to the door the entire time. And as soon as the witch said that I . . . when she said what I was, you wanted to get away from me. Well, now's your chance. Go. I don't need you." Corinne's eyes began to sting with tears, so she blinked them back and stared Dru down while she waited to see what her friend would do.

Dru looked from Corinne to the brothers, and then back to Corinne again. She clenched her fists. "Everything is happening because of you. You are the one she wants. Not us."

"You don't know what you're talking about, Dru," Corinne said.

"I wish we had never met. I wish I had never even laid eyes on you!" Dru ran through the waves toward her village. Her long hair blew behind her.

"You pushed her away," Bouki said to Corinne. "Why did you have to go and do that?"

Corinne took one look at Malik's sad face as he watched Dru run off, and she slumped over with her hands balled into fists on her knees. The tears that she had tried to hold back flowed down her face.

"You can go too," Corinne said. "I would get away from this mess if I could."

"That's exactly why we are staying," Bouki said. "You can't do everything yourself."

"I don't have any choice. My papa can't take care of me anymore. I have to take care of him. There's no one else to do it."

"No, there's one less," Bouki said. "You had three of us. Now you have two."

"You see what happened to my papa. You heard what the witch said. The people around me, the ones who try to protect me, they always get hurt. Even the witch. Who knows what will happen next? Don't you see? I have to work alone."

Malik shook his head.

"What would you like me to tell her, brother?" Bouki said, sounding exasperated. "She wants to go it alone. It's not like I can force her to let us help."

"It's better this way, Malik," Corinne said. "You'll be safe."

Malik shook his head again and stared at her with determination.

Bouki tried to ignore him. "So what are you going to be able to do by yourself, then?" he asked.

Corinne pulled herself up and took a deep breath. "I'm going to do exactly what I should have done in the first place. I'm going to climb the cliff and get my mama's necklace back."

"And then what?"

"You should have seen the look on Severine's face when she touched that stone and it burned her hand. There is something about it. I'm going to figure it out."

"What if that doesn't work? Better to fight it out like we did last night. It's the only way."

"It isn't, Bouki. I know the stone will help. I can just feel it inside me, like the witch said. When I had the necklace, I felt strong. I don't anymore. And why would Severine take it away if it wasn't important? It's the last night and my last chance, so it's time for a real plan. Severine knows exactly what she's doing. By dark tonight, we need to know exactly what we're doing too. And my mama's necklace is step one." She gave the boys a firm nod.

Malik clapped her back in agreement.

Corinne gazed out at the water. "I will need to row out to the cliff. But that fisherman, Victor, he will try to stop me if he sees me. The others might too." Corinne looked at Bouki and Malik.

"What's that look?" Bouki asked. "What do you want us to do about a whole village full of fishermen?"

Malik nudged his brother.

"All right, we can distract the fishermen," Bouki said. "We will find a way."

Excitement tingled on Corinne's skin, from her toes all the way up to her scalp, now that they had a plan. But the weight of the events of the day felt heavy inside her. She could not imagine going it alone. Tears burned in her eyes again. "Thank you," she said.

Bouki patted her on the shoulder. "It would help more if there were three of us." He looked down the coast. Dru was long gone.

Corinne's jaw tightened. "She wanted to go," she said, but her eyes flicked down the coast too. "Anyway, she has a whole family who will be sorry if something happens to her."

"Yet another advantage of being on your own," Bouki replied.

Each syllable of "on your own" pricked at Corinne's heart. But she had to concentrate on what needed to be done. "So how are you going to distract the fishermen?"

Malik pointed to his feet, then made a low peak over his head with his hands.

Bouki smiled and nodded. "Don't worry. We have an idea."

I think he is going to distract him by diving in the water and pretend to be a fish.

< 174 >

29

Disguised

While everyone in the villages was still cleaning up from the night before, Bouki went over to a clothesline behind a house and pulled off a pair of long men's pants. Then he and Malik crossed through some fields to the other side of the island and into their cave. Bouki whittled dry coconut husks into sandals with backward feet. Malik put on the long pants. With the sandals on, too, he looked just like a douen.

"One last thing," Bouki said. He took some dried coconut leaves and wove them into a round hat with a point in the middle for his brother to wear. It was deep enough to cover down to his chin.

Malik walked around with his arms in front of him and whined.

"You don't need to see anything," Bouki explained. "I'll be dragging you the whole time." He cut open two fresh coconuts that they had picked up at the beach earlier in the day. He gave one to his brother, and they drank the sweet coconut water and ate the white jelly in silence.

"It's time to go," Bouki said when they had finished.

Malik's stomach growled.

"Nothing else tonight, brother. This is war. There's no time to eat during war."

Malik whimpered.

"Tomorrow those things will be gone and Corinne's father will bring us the biggest fish in his catch. It will be so big, it will fill us up for three days."

Malik held his stomach and moaned.

"Would you rather have nothing in your belly for one day, or be the thing in a jumbie's belly?"

Malik dropped his hands to his sides and puffed out his chest.

"All right then, brother, let's go."

what will happen next?

30

The Seed

Corinne needed to give the brothers time to get ready. She went to her house, hoping to find that something had changed and there was some way to get in and save her father. The vines seemed even more tightly wrapped around the house, so that it was impossible to see anything past them. She circled, looking for some chink that led inside, but there was no visible opening. And as she moved, the vines shifted, as if they were watching her.

Corinne left reluctantly and made her way toward the sea. The sky burned orange—her mama's favorite time of day—and for a moment, she remembered her mama's smiling face, and a flicker of happiness lit up inside of

< 177 >

her. She wanted to get started. Where were those boys? They needed to hurry. She found a thick grove of coconut trees and hid among them. The tide was in, and the waves pushed foamy brine around her, tugging at her hands and feet, trying in vain to pull her into the sea. She felt the last rays of the sun on her skin and the cool water as it lapped her body. A song her mama used to sing drifted into her mind:

La Siren, la balenn,
Mon chapeau tombe a la mer!
La Siren, la balenn,
Mon chapeau tombe a la mer!

But Corinne knew that there was no mermaid or whale that would come to help her as they did in her mama's song. If the plan was to work, it was mostly up to her alone.

Corinne shoved her hands into her pockets, hoping she had put some fruit in there. But all she came up with was the witch's seed. Only now, instead of just two halves of a seed, there was a little green shoot sprouting from one side and a spiderweb-thin root shooting out of the other.

Corinne held up her palm to get a better look. She frowned at the little plant that had suddenly appeared. Then she snorted in disgust. The witch's magic was strong enough to make this broken seed grow, but she had still refused to help Corinne fight Severine and the other jumbies. Corinne tossed the plant into the surf. A wave brought it back to her.

"Papa was right. The sea doesn't keep anything."

With the sound of her voice, the plant grew a little more. Before Corinne could take a closer look, another wave pulled the tiny plant back out to sea.

I think the boys will do something about it. And corinne will like sneew

< 179 >

31

The Boys' Plan

Malik stumbled behind Bouki in his douen costume. Bouki parted the bushes and helped his brother through so no one would see them before they had a chance to create their distraction. The scent of freshly baked loaves was strong as they passed the bakery. Malik paused, but Bouki shuffled him along. He led Malik past the nearly empty market and edged the road toward a small patch of trees near the dry well, across from the mahogany forest. They needed to get close enough to the fishing village so everyone would hear them scream, but far enough to get them all away and give Corinne her chance.

Someone small appeared on the bend and walked

< 180 >

toward them. When Bouki stepped out to greet her, Dru jumped back with surprise.

"What are you doing here?" he asked.

"I was looking for you."

"No, you're looking for Corinne," Bouki corrected. "She isn't with us. She's going to climb the cliff to get her mother's necklace."

"You let her go?" Dru asked. "No one can climb that cliff." Her hair had been rebraided, and now she unbraided and rebraided the ends of it again.

Bouki shrugged. "Who could stop her? We're her distraction so the fishermen won't get in her way." He waved to Malik, who stepped out from behind the tree.

Dru gasped. "How did you do this?"

"My ingenuity," Bouki said proudly.

Malik kicked him.

"Ow! Well, okay, it was a joint effort." He rubbed his shin. "We're going to pretend that I captured my brother back from the douens. Everyone from the village will come running. That will give her some time to push out to sea."

"But there are jumbies in the forest," Dru said. "What about them? If she makes it to the top of the cliff, won't they come out of the forest to get her?" She bit her lip.

"What else can we do? There are only two of us."

"I'll do it. I'll make sure nothing will be looking toward the cliff. No one will see her."

"Alone? How?"

"I'll think of something. She needs my help," Dru said.

"Even though she's part jumbie?" Bouki asked. "What would your mother say?"

Dru said nothing. She only unbraided and rebraided her hair.

"She'll be killed climbing the cliff," said Bouki, "and you'll be killed going into the forest alone, and we'll be kidnapped by the douens and never seen again. This is an excellent plan."

"At least we would have tried," Dru said.

Bouki smiled with approval and looked at Dru as if he was just seeing her for the first time, and liked what he saw. "Well, we better get to it, then. The sun is nearly gone. The half-jumbie will need her distraction soon," Bouki said.

Malik sighed. The smell of warm bread drifted to them on the wind. Bouki was sorry that he would never steal from the baker again. And he shuddered to think of what douens ate for dinner.

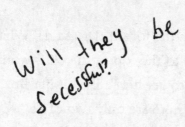
Will they be secessful?

< 182 >

32

Leaving

As soon as Dru came back home, her mother ushered her to the bedroom for safety. Dru stood alone in the middle of the sleep mats and blankets as her family moved in the front room, boarding up the windows and doors. It would be dark soon, and the jumbies would return. The hair on Dru's arms stood out. Her fingers felt cold and numb. But she knew she wasn't just going to stand there while everyone—even her friends—fought.

While the rest of her family secured the front room, Dru changed into one of her brother's shirts and pants. She grabbed some matches and quietly dislodged the two wide floorboards near her mat that she often used to stash things she did not want her siblings to tease her about. She dropped beneath the house, where there was just enough space to lie flat. She crawled out to the side and into the open air. Her heart beat fast. She didn't want to think about what her mother's face would look like when she discovered that her youngest child had disappeared.

Will she get to corinne in time

33

Stepping In

The brothers faced the forest. "Well, brother," Bouki said. He turned to Malik.

Malik extended his hand and Bouki shook it solemnly. They took one last look at each other and stepped into the trees.

I think tracey made these couple Chapters short because alot is going to happen.

< 185 >

34

Firewood

Dru clenched a handful of matches in her fist. Her brother's shirt hung to her calves and her braid had snagged on a nail beneath the house and come loose again. She made her way through the sugarcane fields to the edge of the forest. There she picked up small dry twigs and branches and gathered them up in the hem of the shirt. She looked for an opening in the trees and closed her eyes for a moment to steady her nerves before she entered. Dru navigated through the dark forest with the tips of her toes and fingers. Even though her blood pumped loud in her ears, she kept going. She needed to get as far in as she dared so the small fire she planned to set would cause just enough commotion to surprise the jumbies and the villagers. Her legs trembled as she went on.

35

Nothing

The brothers didn't need to go far into the forest. They stopped at the first line of trees, far enough in that it would look like they had been taken, but close enough to the road to get out fast. As soon as they found a spot to stop, they noticed something strange about the forest. There was no sound or movement around them. It was as if every single creature had disappeared. The sound of nothing at all filled their ears like dry cotton. The brothers strained to hear even the wind in the leaves. Bouki sensed that the jumbies were waiting for them to make their move. He looked at his little brother. Malik puffed his chest out to show he was brave and nodded once. Bouki held his fist out and counted *one, two,* and *three* on his fingers. On the third finger, they both screamed into the night.

The forest awakened.

I think it means like the jumpies screams shaked everything.

< 189 >

36

Pushing Off

Corinne's heart beat out the moments till the brothers' signal would arrive. She watched the fishermen pull their boats in and set their nets to dry. Her muscles tensed. She strained her ears. With the boats moored, the fishermen moved toward their houses. If the boys didn't create their distraction soon, it would be too late. It had to be now, while the men were still outside. Corinne was just about to quit waiting when she heard Bouki and Malik scream.

The fishermen ran toward the sound. Corinne waited for their footsteps to die off in the distance, and then she dashed in the opposite direction to her father's boat.

The tide was going out again, pulling everything back into the sea. Corinne pushed as the tide pulled and got her father's boat into the first small waves.

"If you're in the sea, Grand-père, I could use your help tonight," she whispered. The only answer was the sound of a gentle splash from the waves. Corinne pushed harder, and the boat pulled free of the sand and began to bob in the waves. Corinne jumped inside and pulled one of the oars out to paddle. But as she got away from land, the wind began to work against her. It pushed her toward a shallow spit that threatened to snag the boat. She rowed as fast and as hard as she could, but the shore was not getting any farther away.

"Please!" Corinne called out.

Suddenly the wind changed direction and began pushing the boat out to sea. Corinne turned parallel to the shore and sliced through the waves. High on the cliff, the stone from her mama's necklace reflected the last shards of sun and kept her on a direct path.

What will happen next?

37

Striking the Match

Dru thought she heard Bouki and Malik scream. The sound was tiny and distant, but the night was so quiet that it was possible their cry might have carried for miles. She dropped her bundle of twigs in a pile. Then she worked quickly to clear out a path around it. She had seen her father clear the land around the cane fields every year before he set them on fire at the end of the season. It kept the fire where he could control it. Satisfied with the small circle she made around her twigs, Dru crouched on the ground and tried to strike a match. But every match was damp from the sweat in her hand. As she worked, she heard something moving among the trees. Finally, one of

< 192 >

the matches lit, and in its tiny flame she saw a figure coming closer. Then she heard the rattle of chains.

Dru whimpered and dropped the match. It lay smoking on the forest floor. She crawled backward into a thick
bush and cowered. There was nowhere to go, and the
space she had cleared meant there was nothing between
her and the creature moving toward her but the few twigs
she had found. She pressed back as far as she could go before she realized that she was caught in the branches of a
stinging nettle. The branches of the bush hooked her shirt
and hair and the leaves stung at her hands. The more she
struggled, the more she was caught. Above her, the moon
rose and shone on a fly caught in a spider's web between
bright red balisier flowers. It also struggled to break free,
but neither fly nor girl was successful.

I think the
Layahoo is comming to
save her.

38

The Cliff

The sounds in the villages were now too far away to reach Corinne on her boat. She was close to the cliff, where the water roared and beat the rocks at its base. The closer she got, the choppier the waves became. Beneath the little yellow boat and the silver-black water, currents bashed against hundreds of sharp rocks that jutted up just beneath the surface of the sea. Corinne stopped rowing and allowed the boat to be pushed by the turbulent surf. She used one oar to push away from any jagged rocks that might split the boat. The closer the boat got to it, the more impossibly large the cliff grew. The light was almost gone, and Corinne began to shiver.

It wasn't much farther now.

39

The Douens Fight

E ven though the brothers couldn't see much of anything, they could hear things closing in on them from
all sides. They turned and ran toward the road, toward the
sound of people coming to see what had happened to the
screaming children.

"Did you hear them? Where are they?" the booming
voice of Hugo asked above the crowd that had gathered at
the edge of the forest.

"They're in there!" said Victor.

"They got him!" Bouki shouted as he got near the
road. "They made my brother into one of them!"

Bouki and Malik burst through the trees. Malik did the
best he could to show off his douen feet and to hold on to

the hat on his head. The people came to the road quickly and held up their weapons, ready to attack Malik.

Bouki hadn't thought of this.

"We've lost enough children to these jumbies!" Laurent's mother shouted. "No more!" She stomped toward the boys.

"That one is their last!" Victor said as he came up beside her.

More people came out of their houses, each one carrying some kind of weapon: a garden rake, a large piece of driftwood, stones the size of fists. They all made their way toward the brothers.

Bouki stood in front of Malik and screamed, "Don't hurt my brother!" He knocked Malik to the ground to show them that Bouki's feet were not real, but the adults pressed in closer.

Malik threw himself over his brother and covered both their eyes with his hands. But after a few moments, he peeked through his fingers and saw what the adults were really after—a band of douens standing behind them on the edge of the forest with weapons of their own.

The brothers scrambled out of the way of the fighting and crawled through legs to escape.

Just as they reached the edge of the crowd, Bouki turned back to his brother with a satisfied grin to help him up. But a little jumbie man was right behind Malik. Bouki grabbed Malik's arm quickly, but the douen caught Malik's other arm and Bouki's leg in a vicious grip. It dragged the brothers back between the trees. The fighting adults never noticed. In seconds, all that was left of the brothers was one fake coconut husk foot and the small straw hat.

< 197 >

40

Rough Water

Waves crisscrossed and slapped against each other and the sides of Corinne's boat. The choppy water sprayed salty foam high above her. Corinne grew tired from pushing the boat away from rocks. She couldn't avoid them all. The boat scraped along sharp edges and cracks appeared everywhere in the wood. The waves grew stronger. The boat was pushed in every direction. Corinne sat on her knees, working the oar to avoid destruction while the sea crashed over her and stung her eyes.

She shivered, soaked to the skin, and her arms ached. The base of the cliff was still too far away. Now the boat was heading straight for a large, jagged rock. Corinne moved to the front to try to push away from it, but the boat was moving too fast. She screamed.

In the moonlight, Corinne thought she saw the silver flash of a huge fish tail hit the side of the boat, shoving it out of the way of the rock at the last moment. She wiped saltwater from her eyes to see better, but the creature was gone. Was it real or her imagination? She felt the boat being pushed by some unseen force, and soon she came to a still channel that led to the base of the cliff. "Thank you, Grand-père!" she said to the waves.

Then Corinne looked at the slippery, foam-flecked rocks that rose to the sky above her.

She longed for a moment to catch her breath, but the moon was already high in the sky. It was time to climb.

She searched the black rock for a foothold or a notch for her hand, but she saw only wet rock and crevices filled with sharp barnacles and pieces of shell. A great wave broke against her and the little boat. She braced herself with the oar and heard it crack and split in two. Water ran down the rocks, revealing crumbled barnacles in a nook. It made just enough space for her hand. She used the jagged edge of the fractured oar to scrape away the bits of barnacle that remained and reached up. As another wave gathered its strength to crash into the boat, Corinne pulled herself up by one hand. The fingers of her other hand found a tiny hold, and she curled her toes to grab on to the slippery rock. Just as she left the boat, the wave crashed down, smashing it. The boat's yellow planks were sucked into an eddy. The boat that let her know her papa was always near had disappeared forever.

Corinne bit her lip and moved upward. The farther she went, the drier the rocks were and the easier to hold. She made sure she had a firm grip in one place before she moved to another. As she neared the top, a smooth, flat rock hovered over her. It jutted out with no place for her hands, the final obstacle to reaching the necklace. Corinne had no choice. She was going to have to jump away from the cliff and grab the edge of it with both hands. If she missed, there was only the briny water and sharp rocks to welcome her below.

She clutched the cliffside, nearly frozen with cold and fear. The wind whipped through her wet hair and clothes. She squeezed her eyes shut and thought about her father, how his eyes had glassed over, unseeing, like the murky surface of a swamp. He needed her. She thought about Bouki and Malik taking on the douens. They needed her. She thought about Dru in her noisy house. She needed her too. But who did Corinne need? Who did she have to turn to now?

Above Corinne, her mama's necklace twisted in the wind and its stone's shiny surface blinked back moonlight. Corinne could just make out its light. Her mama was there. She was almost close enough to touch.

Corinne gathered all her strength, crouched, and

jumped. The fingers of one hand caught the top of the rock, but the other slipped and her leg smacked against the cliff. A flood of warmth spread up through her leg, the same leg she'd cut open just a few days ago. She scrambled and found another grip for her left hand. Then she pulled herself up. Her leg left a long streak of blood shimmering against the face of the rock. She found a place for her foot and pushed herself over the top of the cliff. She lay on the edge for a while as her heart pounded and her thigh bled.

The sound of fighting in the village echoed on the rocks. The jumbies were busy. Corinne knew that there wasn't much time to figure out her mama's magic. She pushed herself up to stand and limped over to where the necklace dangled. She untangled it from the dead branch Severine had tied it to and turned the smooth stone in her hand. What was it about this stone that had hurt Severine? And why didn't it hurt Corinne? She was a jumbie too. In the moonlight, Corinne saw a few nicks and scratches on the face of the small stone, but there was nothing remarkable looking about it. She squinted, hoping to detect something useful, some writing or an image she had not noticed before that would tell her what she needed to do. But there was nothing.

As Corinne examined the necklace, an old woman stepped out of the forest and onto the cliff. When Corinne looked up, the woman smiled, then shed her skin and burst into yellow flames. Corinne backed up to the cliff's edge. She was trapped.

41

The Lagahoo

Dru tried to stay still in the bush to avoid brushing against the stinging leaves. The lagahoo drew itself up to its full height, with chains clinking around its neck and waist. It turned to the full moon and bared its teeth. Dru held her breath. Even the fly in the spider's web stopped struggling.

Dru covered her eyes, waiting for the lagahoo's teeth to pierce her skin. In the space between her fingers, she glimpsed a small orange glow. Fire. The match she'd dropped had landed on some dry leaves among her twigs. The flame was gathering strength. It caught onto the hairy leg of the lagahoo. The smell of burning fur filled the air.

The lagahoo rushed forward and fell against the bush that had entangled Dru. The force of the crash freed Dru. Only torn bits of her shirt and a few strands of hair were left behind. The fire spread from the lagahoo to the branches of the bush, well outside the clearing Dru had created. Her blood ran cold with horror.

The lagahoo howled and began to tear itself away from the stinging bush. Dru seized a stick and thrust its end into the flame. Despite her fear of causing more damage, it was the only weapon she had. She waved the fiery end at the lagahoo to keep it away from her. The creature snarled at her. Dru poked and jabbed as she tried to remember which direction led home. The lagahoo swiped at Dru and fire lit up its arm. Quickly its upper body was covered in flames.

The lagahoo roared and twisted, trying to escape the fire. Dru dropped the stick and began to run. The lagahoo grabbed a clawful of Dru's hair and pulled, and Dru landed on her back with a thud. Now the creature was completely covered in flames, and it howled in agony. Dru jumped to her feet and ran. The heat of the fire and the scent of burning fur followed her as she raced screaming through the forest. Finally, she reached the open air and moved as fast as she could through the field toward her house. The burning smell stayed close.

When Dru made it to her village, her family and neighbors stood in the middle of the road, their horror-filled faces lit by the orange glow of the fiery creature. But when Dru looked back, there was nothing behind her. There was just the forest in the distance, consumed in orange flames, and the burning smell, too close to be the forest. Cold water poured over Dru, and then her mother's arms held her tight. Dru was the one who had been on fire. She reached up to touch her hair, but found only wet ash. Her lovely hair had been burned.

I think the dahin is going to meet the bor brothers

42

Captured

Bouki's skin grew moist from the damp air and the fear seeping out of his pores. He looked over at his brother to find that he was slick with sweat too. Another scream pierced the air and bounced off the trunks of the trees around them. The douen that dragged them was joined by several others. They called to each other through the trees.

"Oh! Oh, oh, oh, oh!"

"Kick, brother!" Bouki shouted. Together the boys kicked as hard as they could, but neither could free themselves from the douen's grip. It was like being trapped in stone.

A moment later, the scent of fire came in on the wind and the douens all stopped to sniff the air. Then the sound of feet running, bellies slithering, and wings beating rose up like a wave.

The douen let go of the two boys and ran on its clumsy backward feet to the others. The little jumbie completed a circle that surrounded Bouki and Malik. Bouki scrambled to his feet and pulled Malik up to face the tiny band of spirits. They were small like babies, but their muscles were tough like those of grown men.

The douens closed in. One of them began to whistle a little song, calm and pleasant, despite the commotion around them. Then they all joined in. It was sweet and low and seemed familiar to Bouki. He puckered his mouth into an *O* to join them.

Just as Bouki took a breath to whistle, Malik clapped his hand over Bouki's mouth. Malik shook his head and put one finger to his lips. Bouki understood. This was how the douens trapped children. This was the magic they used to turn children into jumbies like themselves. It had happened to Dru's friend, Allan, and if Malik hadn't figured it out, he would have been next.

The douens whistled louder and moved in.

Malik pointed to something that looked like a path. Then he pointed up in the air. Bouki nodded again. As soon as the douens got close enough, the boys leapt over the jumbies' heads and made for the trail. A loud thud made them look back.

Hugo's large broken pallet had come down on the head of one of the jumbies. "Go!" he shouted at the boys. They both took off running. Behind them, Bouki heard Hugo beating the little men back and then a crack, like wood breaking.

The boys had not gotten very far when Hugo's large arms scooped them up. Bouki felt squashed under Hugo's arm, but he didn't complain. Hugo dodged high roots and low branches. Bouki was surprised that carrying two boys did not seem to slow Hugo down. Bouki looked behind and saw the douens helping up their fallen brothers. But they were far enough away from the little jumbies. Bouki, Malik, and Hugo were safe.

I think the douens will go and capture them.

43

Grow

The soucouyant moved closer and closer, backing Corinne right to the edge of the cliff. A burst of wind whipped around them. It threw the soucouyant's flames higher into the sky and made the jumbie pause and turn. At once, it moved back to the skin it had left on the ground. It was an old woman again. The jumbie sniffed at the smoke that had arrived with the breeze, then returned to the trees. Just then, clouds moved in front of the moon and plunged the night into deep darkness. Corinne brought her mama's necklace to her pounding heart and saw a faint orange glow around it.

Corinne held the necklace up, and it glowed brighter.

Inside there was a small round object. When she shook it, there was a tiny rattle. All the years she had worn it, nothing had ever rattled inside. There was no visible opening, no crack. The clouds moved away from the moon, and the stone stopped glowing. Corinne could see there was only one way to find out what was inside.

She placed the necklace on the ground and picked up a sharp rock. Her fingers trembled. Tears streamed down her face as she thought about destroying the one thing her mama had left her. She held her breath and brought the pointy edge of the rock down. The stone cracked. Orange sparks shot out from its center. Corinne bashed it again. This time, the stone broke apart and a small seed spilled out.

An ordinary orange seed, dry and shriveled.

Corinne had believed the necklace was the key to stopping Severine. But a seed was not magic. It was . . . Corinne couldn't think. She was tired, and her leg throbbed with pain. A cry tumbled out from the pit of her stomach and she crumbled to the ground. Her tears ran along the dirt toward her mama's seed.

The third night was coming to an end. Severine's magic would take hold and Corinne's father would be lost forever.

"Do you think I'm stupid?"

Corinne looked up. Severine stood at the edge of the trees, only she was no longer the beauty who had enchanted everyone at the market. She was long and thin like the branches of an old, rotting tree. Her green cloth wrapping flapped in the wind. Her eyes glowed like yellow flames.

Severine stepped closer, slowly, like an animal stalking prey. "I knew you would try to get that." She pointed a thin, gnarled finger at the broken stone with the seed lying next to it. "And look what you found. A seed? What are you going to do? Throw it at me?" Severine laughed, but she kept an eye on the shriveled little seed.

A large beast appeared next to the jumbie. Its entire body was a dull gray. Even its eyes looked as if they were covered in cobwebs. The beast was wearing clothes like a man, but it lumbered as it walked and sniffed at the air like an animal.

"Mama, what do I do?" Corinne whispered to the broken stone. "Tell me what to do."

"Don't cry," Severine said, syrupy sweet. "Everything isn't lost. You would be very happy with us. I am all that is left of your mother. With me, you can know what she was truly like."

Corinne looked at the destroyed stone. Its black and orange shards glinted in the final rays of moonlight.

"You are nothing like my mama," Corinne muttered. She pulled herself into a tight ball and didn't move.

The witch told me I would lose something, Corinne thought. *My father, my friends, or my freedom. She was right.* Corinne was blinded by tears. *Because I chose to fight to save all three, I could lose everything. What else is there to do but lie here and wait for whatever happens?*

The tears that streamed down Corinne's cheeks had formed a tiny, muddy pool around the seed. The seed trembled. Then it split open at the bottom and a tiny shoot of the palest green emerged from it and rooted itself into the ground.

Corinne blinked. This was not the witch's magic. It was her own. She glanced at Severine, who did not seem to notice what had happened. Corinne sat up and wrapped one of her legs in front of the seedling to hide it from Severine. As she did, she grunted from the pain of her injured thigh, and the seed sprouted a thin green shoot toward the sky.

The wind moved through the trees, and within the sound of softly rustling leaves came a whisper that said: *A seed is a promise, a guarantee. Plant it and watch it grow.* It was her mama's voice, exactly as it had been, kind and gentle, like the wind through leaves.

"Oh," Corinne whispered, and the little sprout doubled in size in response to her voice. She had heard her mama, and now she knew what she had to do. She moved into a crouching position, ready to defend the little plant if needed.

The wind shifted and a stronger scent of fire surrounded them. *Whatever the boys did is getting worse,* Corinne thought. Severine and the beast beside her turned toward the scent. In that moment, Corinne saw her opportunity to escape. With a fire in the forest, she would be the last thought in the minds of the jumbies, who would be trying to put out the fire to save their home. But running away would leave the tiny tree defenseless, and Severine would claim it and whatever magic it held for her own use.

Corinne rose. Should she run or stand her ground?

She planted her feet as firmly as the little orange tree. Severine finally noticed the sapling.

"Well, I see you figured out how to use your mother's magic," Severine said. "Pity it's nothing that can stop me from getting rid of those people you love so much."

"Please grow," Corinne whispered to the tree.

The tree stretched to her knee. Soft branches uncurled from its trunk and delicate leaves unfurled toward the sky.

"Grow," Corinne said again, louder.

In response, the tree grew in earnest. It reached her waist and the trunk and branches began to harden. Corinne grunted as she jumped out of its way. The tree continued to grow, and two blossoms appeared and dropped off. Full, ripe oranges sprouted in their place. The scent of them was irresistible. Corinne reached for one without thinking and sank her teeth into it, rind and all. The orange juice burst into her mouth, and it was the sweetest thing she had ever tasted in her life. She reached for the second one, but Severine swatted Corinne out of the way and took the orange herself. With one bite, her eyes lit with pleasure.

"No!" Corinne cried.

The tree grew again. More flowers bloomed. More oranges ripened.

Severine reached out and grabbed them. Corinne tried to stop her, but Severine threw her backward toward the forest. Corinne skidded and crashed into a pair of sturdy legs. She looked up to see Severine's creature just standing there, watching the scene in silence, the moon glowing off its grayish skin. On its left hand was her father's gold wedding ring.

"Papa?" Corinne asked. Whatever Severine had done to drain him of who he was had also leeched the color from his hair and skin, leaving him almost as pale as the moon. Corinne tried to get her papa's attention, but he was Severine's beast now and kept his eyes transfixed on his mistress.

Severine reached into the little tree, gobbling up every orange as fast as her long hands could pick them. She laughed with glee. She spat out seeds, and orange juice ran down her hairy face. The insects that lived on Severine's body gathered wherever the sticky juice dripped. The ground beneath the tree was soon littered with seeds and empty orange peels and insects that got scraped off Severine's body as she climbed through the branches.

In the east, the sky began to turn pink. In minutes,

the sun would come over the horizon and the third night would be over.

"I've lost," Corinne said to herself.

The tree shot upward again. Severine was pulled up as she held on to an orange. She dangled for a moment but soon grabbed another branch as it grew out. She found a thicker branch to sit in and reached for yet another handful of oranges. Corinne snatched up a rock and got ready to throw it at Severine. But Pierre caught her hand and twisted it until she dropped the rock on the ground.

"Papa, please!" she cried. "It's me, Corinne!"

The tree grew upward again. There were now so many oranges that full, ripe ones rained down and rolled all over the ground. A few stopped at Corinne's feet. Corinne could not resist them. She reached for one, but the beast beat her to it. Corinne kicked at the beast, thinking only of the taste of that juicy, sweet orange. The beast howled and squeezed the orange in anger. Orange juice burst into their faces. It howled.

Corinne screamed.

The tree shot up again. The ground shook as the roots of the orange tree burrowed deeper into the cliff. A crack opened where the earth met the trunk of the tree and split to just a few feet from where Corinne and the beast stood. Both oranges and insects fell in.

Corinne stepped away from the crack. She looked up

at Severine, who was still devouring oranges. "Grow!" Corinne shouted.

The tree grew more and the crack widened.

"Grow!" she cried again.

The tree expanded and the crack became wider still.

"Shut up!" Severine commanded.

Corinne smiled. "Gr—"

Pierre put his hands over Corinne's mouth. She stamped on his feet and struggled to get free but it was no use. Fishing out on the sea had made her father a strong man, and now that Severine had changed him, he was even stronger. Corinne looked at the fallen oranges. She brought her foot down on a large one and turned her face away as the juice flew right up into Pierre's face. He howled again and loosened his grip long enough for Corinne to pull away. Corinne grabbed another orange and threw it right at her father's face. It burst on his forehead, and the juice ran down into his mouth. Pierre stopped growling. Corinne saw the gentleness returning to her father's eyes. A spark of hope ignited in her.

"Grow!" she shouted.

The tree reached a magnificent height, and hundreds of oranges rained down and bounced and rolled around Corinne and Pierre. The cliff was covered in crawling insects, white blossoms, and pungent fruit. The crack widened and the ground rumbled as pieces of rock began to break away from the top of the cliff and fall into the sea. The tree tilted over the cliff as more and more rocks fell.

Severine stopped eating long enough to look down at the surf crashing beneath her. Another rock broke free and fell with a loud splash into the water. Severine's hands gripped the branch she was on. Then she eased one leg onto a lower branch. The tree shook, and she froze again. Corinne held her breath. Any sudden movement could shake the tree from the cliff. Severine moved again, carefully working her way to the branch below. But when she got there, another orange ripened just near her fingers. Corinne tensed. Severine licked her lips and pulled the fruit and the branch with it. When the fruit broke free, the branch swung back and the force of it shook another rock loose.

Severine turned to Corinne. "Stop it. Make it stop!" she yelled. And then her voice softened. "Corinne?"

Corinne looked at the jumbie. Severine's voice had the same gentle tone that she remembered from her mama. It unlocked the sounds that had been silent for so long. Corinne's memories rushed at her like a flood, washing her with the gentle words that had taught her to walk, to plant things, to be kind.

Severine called to Corinne again, and Corinne ran toward the voice that sounded so much like her mother's. The tree leaned out of the crack and hung over the cliff. She didn't know how to stop it from falling.

"Help me!" Severine called.

Pierre leapt to her rescue. When he landed, another rock dislodged and fell into the sea and the tree tilted down farther. Now it was almost horizontal to the ground. Severine gripped the branches with her arms and legs. Her insects abandoned her, crawling out of her body and onto the cliff. Pierre got near the edge and reached for Severine but she would not let go of the tree.

"Jump!" Corinne called out.

The tree grew again as Severine crouched and tried to jump up and out of the branches, reaching for Pierre's hands. As she did, the first light of the morning peeked over the horizon. Corinne gasped as Severine's twiggy fingers reached toward Pierre. The tree grew longer and tilted even more. The tips of Severine's fingers grazed Pierre's. Corinne bolted forward. The force of her body knocked Pierre out of the way and sent him rolling from the edge and away from the morning light. Severine flailed and managed to grab on to the rock face, but her green cloth snagged in the branches of the tree. She tugged at the cloth. The tree tipped again and tore away from the cliff. A branch swept her hand off the rock, and Severine spiraled down, down, down with the tree toward the sea far below.

Corinne stood at what was now the new edge of the cliff. Below, waves crashed over Severine and the tree as the sea claimed them, and then crashed and crashed again as they always had and always would, as if the terrible jumbie had not just disappeared beneath their foam. Sunlight blinded Corinne, and she turned toward her father. He stared at her from the shadows.

The sun had come up on the third day.

Pierre growled at Corinne, his teeth sharp and dripping with saliva.

She couldn't back away. There was nowhere to go. "Papa, please. You know me. I'm your daughter."

Pierre snarled and moved toward her.

Corinne said, "Saltwater runs in your veins and mud runs in Mama's and Grand-père is king of the fish-folk, and I'm . . . I'm not afraid of anything!" Sunlight inched steadily toward her father along the ground. Just before the first light reached him, the beast lunged at her.

"No, Papa!" Corinne screamed and threw an orange at his gaping mouth.

She sank to her knees and wept as sunlight lit the entire cliff. The witch was right. She could not win.

But then a cold, pale hand touched her face.

Corinne looked up. "Papa?"

In the warm sunlight, Pierre was beginning to look like himself again, strong and kind, not like the mindless, snarling creature that he had been moments before.

Corinne grabbed another orange and squeezed the juice into his mouth. Slowly Pierre's face returned to its familiar sun-kissed brown.

Corinne fed her father another orange, and another.

His hair turned black again. He was still coming back. And at last, there was Corinne's papa kneeling beside her.

"I'm so sorry, Corinne!" He kissed the tight braids on his daughter's head like he used to every morning.

Corinne hugged him tight.

Together they looked down into the sea where Severine had disappeared. Nothing remained on the water's surface but a few floating branches and bobbing oranges.

Now they had a new problem. The forest near the cliff was ablaze.

"How will we get through?" Corinne asked.

Pierre looked to the sea and pointed to a single dark cloud. "Just wait," he said. Moments later, the rain began.

falling actions

what will happen next?

44

For Keeps

Corinne and her father filled their pockets with as many oranges and seeds as they could carry and turned to go home. "We'll get lost, Papa," Corinne said.

"But we have to try, don't we?"

As they stepped toward the trees, a douen appeared and pointed the way. Pierre stiffened.

"I think it's trying to help us, Papa."

Still, Pierre's eyes glittered like a rough sea. "We can't be sure," he said.

"We have to try," Corinne reminded him.

Pierre shifted Corinne to his other side, away from the jumbie, and together they followed the path. A few steps into the forest, the trees were so close together that they did not know where to go next. Another douen appeared and pointed the way. As they went, more jumbies stepped in to show them the way home.

Some bowed their heads slightly as Corinne and Pierre passed. Others watched them with wary eyes, but did nothing to stop them from going. One lagahoo reached out to Corinne with an expression that resembled a smile. Corinne squeezed Pierre's hand tight, and they both stopped in their tracks. The lagahoo looked down at Corinne's bleeding leg and whispered something. A moment later, a douen came out from some undergrowth and put something against the cut. Almost instantly, the pain was gone. Pierre bowed his thanks.

When Corinne and her father finally emerged on the road, a crowd of villagers stood silent before them. The witch stepped forward. Dru and the brothers stepped forward too. The three of them were barely recognizable. Bouki and Malik were dressed in clean, untorn clothes and had somehow managed to scrub the color of mud from their hair and skin. It turned out that they were more golden brown than mud red. And Dru! Corinne walked with uncertainty toward her friend. Dru wore a sari, but her braids were gone, and her short, shaggy hair made her look like a fierce little boy.

"What happened?" Corinne asked.

"I set a fire to distract the jumbies," Dru said. "I

< 221 >

cleared the land and everything, but it didn't go the way I planned." Her hands touched her hair and tried to twirl the ends, but there was not much there. She dropped them to her sides. "I was lucky the rain came. It could have been worse."

"You helped me?"

Dru nodded and Corinne could not resist giving her friend a hug.

"And they got a father," Dru said about the boys.

"What father? Who said anything about having a father?" Bouki asked.

"You think I didn't see you coming out of the baker's house this morning?" Dru asked.

"He fed us. We were tired, so we stayed. It was a long night."

"If it wasn't for the ears, I might not have recognized you," Corinne said to Malik. Then she turned to Bouki. "So it's back to the cave tonight?" she asked with a smirk.

Malik winced.

"We are not the baker's children. He is not taking care of us," Bouki said.

"He's been taking care of you for years," Corinne said. "Every night you find food in his bakery for your dinner. Did you think it was a coincidence?"

Bouki and Malik took a sheepish glance over at Hugo. The big man grinned and shifted from one leg to the other like someone caught in a small lie.

< 222 >

The witch hobbled over and pointed at Bouki with her thumb. "I told you before that that one wasn't very smart." She snorted and searched Corinne's eyes. "Well, how did the stone work?"

"It wasn't the stone at all. It was the seed inside it. Just like you showed me. Watch." She held a seed in her hand and put it close to her lips. "Grow."

Almost at once, the seed rocked and split and a tiny green shoot sprouted up.

The witch smiled. "Yes. That is the way," she whispered to herself.

Bouki, Malik, and Dru looked on, astonished. Corinne handed the sapling to Malik.

"But is she gone?" Bouki asked.

Corinne nodded. "She's gone."

"What about the other ones?" Dru asked. "They're still here."

Corinne looked at her papa. "But she's not controlling them anymore," Corinne said. "And they belong to the island. They've been here longer than we have."

Pierre nodded and the white witch smiled at Corinne's words, but a grumble rose from almost everyone else.

"They will come out again," Victor said.

"They took my child!" shouted a woman.

"They killed my husband," said another.

"What about what she did to your father?" Dru asked. "What about the people we lost?"

"That was all Severine," Corinne said. "Just now the jumbies helped us get out of the forest. They helped heal my cut." She pulled away the patch of leaves on her leg to show a wound that looked nearly healed. "Do you see? We have to find a way to live together."

There was more grumbling. Someone picked up a broken branch and smacked it against the palm of his hand. "I'm not going to live here while they still live here," he said. It was Laurent's father. Laurent stood beside him with a fierce scowl, as if he was determined to fight.

"Then you can take your chances in the sea," said the witch.

The faces in the crowd turned hard. Corinne looked at her father to see if he knew what to do. He squeezed her hand gently in his. It gave her courage.

"This island was theirs before we ever knew anything about it," Corinne said in a strong voice. The witch nodded in agreement. "But now we're all here together. It's our home. All of ours."

"They took my friend," Dru said.

"And we have taken their homes," Corinne answered. "Every time we cut down a tree to plant crops, they get pushed back."

Dru bit her lip.

Malik stepped forward with the orange sapling in his hand. He dug a little hole in the ground by the forest and planted it. Then he looked at Corinne. "Grow," he whispered.

Corinne and Dru looked at Malik with shock.

"I don't know why you're so surprised," Bouki said. "I told you, he talks plenty."

Corinne took the orange seeds from her pockets and began to push them into the ground. The witch took some of the seeds and helped. Pierre handed more seeds to Dru, the brothers, and a few others, and they all planted rows of orange trees at the edge of the forest.

Corinne held her hand out to the witch and said, "It's a lot of seeds. I don't think I can grow them all on my own."

The witch took Corinne's hand with her good one. "I can help with this," she said.

"Grow," the half-jumbies said together.

The seeds began to sprout.

A few people in the crowd gasped. The orange trees curved upward. They hardened and turned brown as they grew into each other and formed a solid wall that reached far into the sky. The trees looked beautiful, but more than that, they smelled delicious. The people in the village couldn't resist picking the fruit and eating it on the spot. Only Dru stayed back.

"This isn't going to stop them," she said. Her face was furrowed with worry.

"It's not to keep them in," Corinne said. "It's to keep us out. We've been taking their land. They deserve to survive too."

The sight of the orange trees barring the way jogged

Corinne's memory. "The jumbie weed on my house!" she cried.

"It's dead," Bouki said. "We went to see this morning. But it's going to take a lot of cleaning up."

"If that kind of magic can fall, then so can this," Dru protested. "They will come after us."

"The only time they ever came after us was when we disturbed them," Corinne said. "And when Severine started her war. You even said you had never seen them before."

Dru said, "And when those trees are gone, then what?"

"Maybe by that time we will have found a way to live together." Corinne hugged Dru. "I'm sorry about your friend," she said.

Dru wiped a tear from her cheek. "I'm sorry I said I wished I had never met you. I blamed you for what happened to Allan. I thought you were just like them. I thought you would turn against us and everything would just get worse and worse."

"That's the thing, Dru. There is no *us* and *them*. And anyway, some good things happened," Corinne reminded Dru. "Look at these two!" She gestured at Bouki and Malik in their clean clothes and grinned. Corinne reached out to both of them for a hug.

"Hold on, now. We just got cleaned up. You look like you've been sleeping in mud," Bouki said. "And anyway, we don't hug girls."

Malik made a firm nod. His curly hair bounced around him.

Corinne laughed.

Some in the crowd looked with wonder at the wall of orange trees and others looked at Corinne with suspicion. The pride that Corinne had felt began to fade as some people backed away and others whispered behind their hands. Pierre put his hand on his daughter's shoulder and squeezed.

Corinne felt her chest tighten. She whispered to the witch, "Is this what you meant? Is this what I lose?"

The witch sneered. She yelled out, "Her oranges taste sweet though, eh? None of you are putting them down."

The crowd mumbled to themselves and began to disperse, most with some oranges clutched to their chests.

Corinne didn't watch them go. Her eyes stayed on Dru, who had remained rooted to the spot, looking uncertain.

"Are you going too?" Corinne asked.

Dru reached into her waist and untucked part of her sari, then unrolled it to reveal the wax form of Corinne's mama. Even in the daytime it radiated light from deep inside.

Corinne's heart leapt as she took the statue. "How did you fix this?" she asked.

Dru shrugged. "Just know I'll always be there to help you." She blew a kiss toward Corinne and skipped off to her village.

Corinne sighed with relief.

The brothers nodded to Corinne and followed the baker, walking carefully in their clean clothes and minding all the muddy puddles from the morning's rain. Corinne watched as they steered clear of a large one but missed seeing a little frog that sat squat in the middle of the road. Bouki tripped over the quiet little frog and grabbed Malik to catch his balance. Both brothers fell smack into the very puddle they had been avoiding. They sat up sputtering, their new clothes completely covered in mud. Everyone laughed, even the baker, who grabbed the backs of the boys' shirts and pulled them out in one easy lift.

As Corinne wiped tears of laughter from her eyes, she noticed the little frog hop away. Somehow it looked very familiar.

With a broad smile, Corinne showed her father the wax statue. Pierre nodded and gave her his warm, rough hand to hold.

Meanwhile, in the sea, oranges bobbed up and down. Waves pushed hundreds of them onto the shore. They scraped against rocks at the bottom of the surf, which bruised their skin and released their smell. The sharp, sweet scent of oranges filled the air all over the island.

Pierre smelled them and his face turned worried. "The sea doesn't keep anything," he said.

Corinne squeezed his hand. "It kept Grand-père," she

said. "Maybe some things stay in the sea. And you and I stay where we belong. Together."

Pierre managed a smile.

"Let's go home, Papa," Corinne said. "We have jumbie weed to clean up. It's too bad I can't make things un-grow."

"Can't you?" he asked.

The two of them looked at each other, wondering. Then they broke into broad smiles and headed off toward their house.

< 229 >

Author's Note

Jumbie (JUHM-bee) is the name for every bad-think-ing, sneaky, trick-loving creature that comes out at night with the purpose of causing trouble. There are many different kinds of jumbies, from la diabless to churiles, to the douens and lagahoos in this book—and many more. The important thing to remember is to beware of jumbies wherever you go. They love to trick you, and they can dis-guise themselves as *anyone*. It might be your nice neigh-bor Mr. Jeanty, who walks his dog every afternoon when you get home from school. It might be your math teacher Miss Izzard. I hate to say it, but it might even be me.

Your friendly ~~jumbie~~ author,
Tracey Baptiste

P.S. You can learn more about all kinds of jumbies in "Jumbies: A Field Guide," available to download at traceybaptiste.com and algonquinyoungreaders.com. It will teach you how to handle a jumbie if you meet one.

Read on for a sneak peek at new adventures
awaiting Corinne and friends in

Rise of the Jumbies

C orinne La Mer dove through the waves. Streaks of light illuminated the golden sand beneath her and shone on a large pink shell half-buried on the seafloor, just out of reach. She kicked her feet and reached toward it, but just as she got close enough, a pair of dark hands snatched the shell. Bouki grinned. A few bubbles escaped from between his teeth, and he pushed up toward the sun.

"Eh heh!" he said when Corinne joined him over the waves.

"Fine, Bouki. You win," Corinne said.

"Say it," he said. "Say it!"

Corinne rolled her eyes. "You're . . ."

But before she could finish, his little brother swam up behind and yanked the shell out of his hand.

". . . not king of the sea!" Corinne finished. "Looks like Malik is."

Bouki dove after his brother. Corinne swam for shore. They had been in the water for hours. Her fingers were wrinkly and her eyes burned. She dragged herself over to a coconut tree and sat against its curved trunk, sticking her legs straight out in the warm sand. Striped shadows from the coconut leaves danced on her skin and the ground in front of her.

The sand shivered. Corinne felt a tremor go straight through her body. The people on the beach stopped mid-action. But her papa and the other fishermen in their boats were still far out on the water, their nets dragging in the sea. None of them seemed to notice. She looked up at the sky. It was clear and quiet. *Where are the seagulls?* she wondered. The ground shook again. This time, she got up.

"Earthquake!" one of the women shouted.

Corinne looked into the water again. There was no sign of the boys.

"Get out of the water!" another voice yelled.

Mothers with small children gathered them up and ran from shore. Laurent, one of Corinne's friends from the fishing village, rounded up his siblings while his mother came behind with the baby. The second youngest, Abner, stumbled. Corinne reached for him, but his mother pushed Corinne's hand away, and in one swoop, tucked Abner under her free arm.

"Mrs. Duval, I was only trying to help."

Laurent's mother cut a fearful glance at Corinne, and Corinne's face burned with embarrassment.

Maybe it's just the earthquake, Corinne thought. But it wasn't. She had been getting looks like that for months.

Corinne ran toward the waves. "Bouki! Malik!" she shouted.

The boys' heads bobbed up out of the water. They were still fighting over the shell.

"Get out!" Corinne yelled. "Get out of the water!"

At the water's edge, the waves pulled back as if the ocean were being drained.

Bouki and Malik beat a path toward Corinne, but the sea was still pulling them away from shore. Corinne ran forward, toeing the froth at the edge of the waves. She was much farther out than she had been when they were playing. But where there had been water deep enough to swim in, there was now only wet, sucking sand.

"Faster!"

Water splashed on Corinne's toes. The tide was turning. The boys got closer, but so did the sea. Corinne stayed where she was with the water licking at her feet, her ankles, and then surging up to her knees until the brothers were close enough to grab and pull along.

"Run!" Corinne commanded. All three of them took

< 234 >

off toward the hill where she lived. But the waves crashed down around them, washing the sand away and pulling at their feet. One wave had barely turned back when another one overtook it and came at them again. It was the strongest tide Corinne had ever experienced.

There was another rumble. Corinne and the boys scrambled over rocky steps. Loose stones shook away beneath their feet, tripping them until they reached the dirt road. They stopped a moment with their hands on their knees to steady themselves and catch their breath. The ground stopped moving, but the waves kept coming, and they were bringing the fishing boats in fast—right to where they stood. Corinne's papa's yellow boat crashed into other vessels as it rushed toward shore. Her father's eyes found her. He pointed frantically at their house at the top of the hill.

Corinne nodded once and pulled the boys behind her. Malik stumbled and Bouki helped him to his feet.

"Come on, brother," Bouki said.

They continued up the hill and paused near the house to look over the beach, which was now covered in brackish water, tree limbs, and splintered wood. A small brown object, round like a bare head, bobbed by, and for a moment, Corinne's heart stopped. But there were others, green ones, yellow ones—coconuts, Corinne realized with relief—all drifting in the water.

She looked to the pileup of boats that had run aground, but her papa's was not among them.

Tracey Baptiste is the *New York Times* bestselling author of *Minecraft: The Crash* and the Jumbies series. She lived in Trinidad until she was fifteen; she grew up on jumbie stories and fairy tales. She is a former teacher who works as a writer and editor. Visit her online at traceybaptiste.com and on Twitter: @TraceyBaptiste.